BROKEN GIRL

FAÎTE FALLING
BOOK FIVE

MARY E. TWOMEY

MARY E. TWOMEY

Broken Girl

Book Five in the Faîte Falling Series

By

Mary E. Twomey

COPYRIGHT

Copyright © 2017 Tuesday Androsian
Cover Art by Emcat Designs

All rights reserved.
First Edition: July 2017

For information:
http://www.maryetwomey.com

DEDICATION

For my sister, Michelle,

Broken or whole, I love all of your many pieces.

1

SADNESS AND SCRAMBLED EGGS

"You locked me out of your room last night," Kerdik accused quietly over breakfast. His chocolate-colored fitted slacks, crisp white dress shirt and charcoal vest were perfectly in place, making me look that much more disheveled in my jeans and wrinkled t-shirt.

I ate in the stone-floored kitchen with the staff, hoping they'd be normal and go about their day around me, but they ended up speaking in hushed whispers and being on their best behavior. I couldn't tell if they thought I would have a nervous breakdown and start bawling because my *Guardien* and my fiancé were gone, or if they were scared my temper was as sharp as my mother's – the dreaded Morgan le Fae. Or maybe they were terrified of Kerdik, whose displeasure was known to affect whole celestial orbs and throw nature into chaos. Either way, it made for an awkward breakfast, even a whole week after the Untouchables had left. I tried not to think about them, not to miss Link's goofy grin, Madigan's absence of a personality that only I found endearing, and...

I shuddered, reminding myself that I wasn't going to think about *him*. I vowed not even to say *his* name in my mind; it was too painful to hear it. I chewed on the toast, but it felt like sand in my mouth. "My locked door sure didn't stop you from breaking in."

"I was worried about you."

"Nothing to worry about. Sometimes things don't work out. Is what it is." I brushed the crumbs off my white t-shirt and stood. "I'm going back out to help with the wall."

Kerdik rubbed his hands over his face, exasperated with me even though the sun had barely risen. "You're still technically injured. I don't think manual labor is the right call."

"Maybe not, but it's my call. I want to help. There was a whole whorehouse operating right under my nose, but I didn't know a thing about it because I was laying around the mansion like a lazy bum."

"You're not lazy, you're injured!" As his tone rose, the servants scattered, fearful of his swinging rage. Two of the sisters who ran the kitchen, Faith and Mercy, whimpered, shoving each other to get out as quick as they could.

When it was just us on the tall stools at the stone island, I took my dish to the sink. I'd eaten half my breakfast, which felt like one brick too many sitting in my stomach. "Look, I need to keep myself busy, and I don't want to drop the ball on the whole princess thing. Lane should come back to a peaceful region with a wall in place."

Kerdik's nostrils flared. "You're shutting me out. I'm not the one who cheated on you."

I flinched at mention of the crime I'd specifically told my Avalonian BFF not to mention ever again if he valued his testicles. "You're not allowed to psychoanalyze me."

Kerdik raised his eyebrow, pursing his lips. "Being a brat to me isn't going to bring Bastien home."

I washed my dish with jerky movements, fuming. "I don't want him home. You seem to think I'm pining for the man who cheated on me in a whorehouse, who was so drunk, he couldn't lift a helping hand when I was attacked right in front of him. I am not so desperate as to ache over someone like that."

Kerdik stared at my black neck tattoo with unhampered attitude, as only the most intimate of friends could do. He'd laid in bed with me every night since Bastien had gone, so I think we'd achieved that level of closeness that kept me from shoving him when he spoke hard truth I didn't want to hear. "Actually, that's exactly what I think. I think you're waiting for him to come back with some amazing excuse that would make all the wrongs right again between the two of you." He shook his head. "It's not going to happen. He did what men who are unhappy often do. It's nothing more complicated than that."

"Do you want to wear that breakfast?" I steamed,

eyeing his scrambled eggs and berries. My mood had been fouler than my usual cheery, shrug-it-off disposition, but everyone seemed to be giving me a pass. Somehow this only made me more irritable. "I told you that I don't need to hear his name, and there you go, just blurting it out like a foghorn. I know he's gone. I sent him away myself. This is me, moving on."

"You sleep fitfully now, when you do at all. You used to require eight hours a night, but you're barely down for two at a time before you're up and back at that wall. You're shutting out the animals, so your magic's not wearing down as much. You need them. They make you happy." He popped a berry into his mouth. "You called out for Bastien in your sleep again last night when I came in to check on you."

I inhaled sharply, my nostrils flaring at the verbal slap he would have been better off not mentioning at all. Instead of arguing, I scooped up a handful of his warm eggs and smeared them down his cheeks. I examined the sight that was Kerdik a mess, and looked with a satisfied sense of accomplishment at the beautiful picture. "Wow, I didn't think I could smile, but that sure did it. Thanks for being a jerk just so I could make you wear your breakfast."

Kerdik glowered at me, the stone floor beneath us rattling with his temper before he cooled down a few breaths later. "You're welcome. If I didn't mention you being a brat before, it goes double now. And you're not actually smiling, you know, so it wasn't even worth it."

"Oh, it was worth it."

"You haven't smiled in a week. That's not you. What's the point of being near you if there's no *you* left?" He said it as if he expected an answer.

"Then leave! I'm sure you could bunk up with the Untouchables, wherever they are. Or you could go see Lane, who's still not back. Maybe you could go for a walk in the woods where I buried Abraham Lincoln and Hamish. Everyone else makes good use of the front door. Knock yourself right friggin' out, if this isn't the place you want to be."

"This isn't you." Kerdik squinted at me and tilted his head to the side, as if trying to size up something that was more complicated than a broken heart.

I pursed my lips, and then tried to calm down my frustration. Kerdik had actually stuck around, and I was lashing out at him for it. He was right; this wasn't me. I used to know who I was, but I felt like I was banging around against the walls of being too much, and still not enough. I couldn't find my center. I couldn't find me.

I crossed my arms over my chest and leaned on the counter, not wanting Kerdik to be right. "You're getting too I-know-everything about it all. He was my first love, K. It's going to sting for a while." I looked at the eggs I'd smeared on his cheek and winced. "Sorry about making you wear your breakfast."

He used the water he produced from his elemental

magic, and ran his hands down his face, washing off the egg residue. "Do you want to talk about it?"

I shook my head. "I'm going out to the border. Send a magical bunny or singing telegram if you need me."

His nose crinkled. "You're a princess. You don't need to be building walls with a bunch of sweaty men."

I stretched out my back, which was sore from all the tossing and turning I'd done before Kerdik snuck in to cuddle me last night. "What I need is to work through some of this crap, and manual labor is a good way to do that. This is my province, so I should be out working in it. If hard labor is good enough for my subjects, then it's good enough for me."

Kerdik studied my face, and finally sighed. "Fine. If that's what you need, go on and do what you have to. Take Draper with you, okay? And don't work too hard. I mean it. Yesterday was too much, and you know it."

"Sure." Draper had been good about giving me my space after it all imploded. He was antsy without Lane around, so he stuck by my side that much more voraciously. Turns out, we both like to work when we're stressed, so neither of us gave the other one too much grief about it. Dad was well enough to take on most of the royal responsibilities, which was a relief to us both.

Kerdik stood before me and cupped my face, trying to warm my cold places. He pulled back and squinted at me, frustrated with my resigned nature. "Where are you, darling?"

"I'll be out on the border until Dad needs me to sit and hold court with him tonight."

"That's not what I meant."

I shrugged. "I know. I'm not really anywhere. I'll figure it all out. First broken heart. Where's the baby book, am I right? This one deserves a photo op." I ducked away when he tried to kiss my cheek. I didn't want to hurt him, but I saw the fresh wound there all the same. I shook my head, unable to look at him as I tapped my heart. "It's not you. You're perfect. Really, K. Better than I deserve right now. It's me. If you kiss me, it'll make me feel, and I don't want to feel right now. I want to nothing myself into oblivion. I need to be perfectly and utterly nothing."

Kerdik's eyes lit with that fire I'd seen build a cave out of a field in a heartbeat. He jerked me to him in a possessive way I wasn't altogether unfamiliar with, my breasts pushed against his firm chest. It rattled the feelings around inside of me, which was the exact opposite of the nothing I'd asked for.

His lips found mine so quickly, I scarcely knew what to do with myself. His hand pressed on the small of my back so that I was arched against him, my waist mashing to his hips in a way that was altogether carnal and probably not too ladylike. Confusion, indignation and a lust I didn't mean to feel rose up in me as my lips started to revel in the dirty dance they'd been invited to. The kiss was passionate, but lasted only a few agonized seconds. I felt more in those few seconds than I'd allowed myself in an entire week. He ripped a gasp from my mouth, swallowing it and making it his own.

When I finally had the wherewithal to pull away, my shriek was embarrassed. "What the crap, K?"

Then, so fast I almost fell over, Kerdik whirled me around, pressed my back to his chest and snatched an apple off the counter. He held it out in front of me as an ominous belch built up in my belly. I panicked when I remembered the last time we'd kissed, and the blaze that erupted from that carefully contained mess. I tried to slap my hands over my mouth, but Kerdik pinned them both down with an arm around my waist to secure me to him. "Let it come," he whispered, his lips tickling the shell of my ear.

The fire burst out of me much the same as it had before, aiming itself at the apple and toasting it as it lay in his palm. "I'm sorry!" I choked out when the fire died as quickly as it started. I was horrified that I'd hurt him.

"You can't injure me with fire. I'm an elemental, remember?" He moved the apple closer so I could see the crisp outer layer that had browned on one side. He buried his face in my neck, placing a kiss to a spot that was too sensitive to let him near without a shiver running through me. "People who are nothing feel nothing. You are not nothing," he reminded me, his fingers digging into my hip as if he knew how to orchestrate all of my throaty moans. "*You* are my fire."

I finally turned around in his arms, his fervor breaking

through what had been a week of trying to numb everything with work and avoidance. I didn't like my bed without *him* in it. I didn't like the mansion without *him* bumming around, either. There had been an ache in my chest since I'd sent his drunken butt off in a wagon with Link and Mad. With time, it seemed that hole only grew larger.

Kerdik held me, hoping I would break in his arms, but I maintained what little dignity I could scrape together, and remained in his embrace with a quiet demeanor. Finally, I leaned up on my toes and pecked his cheek. "I love you. No more kissing me, though. I'm already a mess. You shouldn't hitch your wagon to a dead horse."

He traced my lips like a man who knew exactly what to do with them. "I'll not apologize for it."

"How unlike you." I managed a... not quite a smile, but a lighter expression nonetheless, and squeezed his side, even though he wasn't ticklish. "See you tonight when you break into my room again." I sniffed his collar, my eyebrows pushing together in faux concern. "Hm. You smell like scrambled eggs. Might want to wash that off of you."

Kerdik was not amused at my joke, his eyes narrowing. "Leave the door unlocked tonight, or risk my displeasure."

"Dum-da-dum!" I sang ominously, mocking his almighty temper as I left.

2

ONE REGION, NOT NINE

I made my way outside just as the sun started to rise in the east, walking down the grassy path half a mile to where the men were building the wall. It was supposed to outline our territory and make us all feel safer. Not sure how much truth there was to the whole being safer part, but it got everyone working together, so I was cool with it.

I did a two-fingered wave to the bowing that always started at the beginning of the work day, and faded to congenial penis jokes about an hour into the job. Draper joined us after his breakfast, kissing my dirty cheek before he started in on mixing more mortar, which was his job of choice. I always saw him making meaningful eye contact with the two men in charge of doling the responsibilities for the day. Montel was about Draper's age, and looked on me with the same kid sister-like affection. Pascal, the foreman, was Montel's father, and treated every man like he needed an extra task to do. I liked Pascal. He kept me nice and busy, and got irritable when I fell behind the guys who were twice my size.

The elders in the area all gave me pitying looks, shaking their heads at me and whispering things like "jilted" and "old maid." Since I was royalty, they had to keep their indignation to a quiet murmur, but it was clear the rumor was that I was defunct, now that Mad had left me and taken his ring back. Pascal didn't care that I was earning myself a fair bit of stigma by being unceremoniously dumped. Pascal cared about the wall only. He was surly, dark-skinned, sweaty and never smiled. Gotta love a bald man who doesn't put on a show.

The sun wasn't too excruciating, but lugging bricks to the border so the masons could spackle them in place made the sweat pour off me faster than I could rehydrate myself. I treated it like a personal fitness session at a gym. The more I sweat, the more I was winning. My body would be killer when Pascal was done training me. There was no play to my days anymore, only the slow, drawn-out punishment I gravitated toward. Each heavy brick grounded me, anchoring me when I felt afloat in my misery.

Unless what was required of me were unintelligible grunts, I was barely able to piece together a conversation when the day ended. I couldn't tell if that was due to the depression, or from doing a hard day's work too many days in a row. Either way, it kept unnecessary conversation away from me.

Since Avalon was the city that never slept, I migrated to the Town Square with Draper and Montel flanking me after we called it a day. I longed to go hole myself up in my bedroom, but Draper was firm that making friends with the locals was part of the royalty gig. Every evening after the sun dipped down, the Town Square was the height of the social scene. Tables were brought out with chairs enough for the weary workers, and the women who'd been baking, cooking, cleaning and setting up their homes came out with a simple feast to welcome their men back from the day's work. There was an appreciation about the people, and a relief that made their merriment even brighter.

I could see the splintering off of provinces that usually happened in small segments as the evening began, but then broke into deeper divides as the night wore on. The lanterns hung on nine poles encircling the Town Square, one for each of the nine provinces. They were painted the signature colors of each one, with our green post standing tallest. They'd been put there as a tribute of unity, but the immigrants from the differing regions used those poles as a talisman, moving their chairs around so they could sit by the province they'd come from, and keep away from the others.

Draper was content to eat with the people from Province 9, since he'd given himself completely to the idea that Lane was his mother, and everything else before her just plain didn't exist. I loved his devotion to us, but the villagers weren't clinging to their poles out of love, but rather the precious fear they adhered to in this new land that they hadn't quite adjusted to yet.

"Oh, he was huge. Huge and grateful," I heard a woman say to her friend. I turned and saw Ruby, the hire-by-the-hour woman Bastien had used to cheat on me. "Bastien the Bold was exactly what I needed to take the edge off. Best lay of my life." Her giggle was shared by her friend, and though the public hadn't known we were together, indignation rose up in me.

Only Ruby hadn't known we were together, so other than taking money for sex, she hadn't done anything wrong. I kept my mouth shut, and let her have her moment in the sun, feeling the shame that came from your guy stumbling into someone else's bed.

For some reason, that evening I'd had enough of the dodgy glances and snotty whispers the factions kept shooting each other from the safety of their poles. A bowl of thick stew was handed to me with a crust from a baguette, and I moved on down the line with the rest of the workers. I stopped my progression to the Province 9 pole, though Draper was waving me over to sit with him. I was finally invited to sit at the cool kids' table. After going so many years as Remedial Rosie, it was a grand gift I didn't dismiss lightly.

I shook my head at my brother and moved to the abandoned center of the Town Square, sitting in the dirt at the base of the platform Madigan had almost killed me on. My squirrel and my bear baby had bled and died on this very stage, and I'd been avoiding it ever since. Sure, Madigan had been conditioned to obey when someone used his trigger word, and in the end, I'd escaped with my life, but my bear was still dead. The loss tapped me on the shoulder whenever I came into the Town Square. The platform gave me all sorts of get-outta-Dodge feels to it that I tried to muscle past as I ladled a spoonful of soup down my gullet.

The whispers ramped up to out and out pointing now, as my scandal spread through the factions like a crowd at a baseball game doing the wave. Odd as I felt eating alone, I knew I had to do something about the separation that was happening right under my nose.

Draper trotted over to me and offered his hand, but I shook my head in response. He frowned down at me, and then crouched to get on my level. "Everything alright, Pumpkin? You don't have to eat here where you almost..." He cleared his throat. "You're torturing yourself being so near the stage. You don't need to do that."

I started tearing off bits of bread and tossing them in my stew. I kept my head down so he didn't have to see just how rattled I was over being so near the platform. Hamish and Abraham Lincoln had died there at the hands of my fake fiancé. I could still hear my bear's last, agonized howl as he gave his life to protect mine. I cleared my throat and tried to straighten. "I can't take it anymore. Everyone's together, but we're not one nation yet. If Morgan pounces again, there's no guarantee they'll all fight together. We can't even get them to eat together. I don't belong to a province. I belong to Avalon, I guess. So I'm going to eat here with anyone who feels the same way. They're all displaced, just like I am. But they're still clinging to anything familiar, so they don't have to admit the old ways are over. They have the chance at a new start, but part of them still isn't taking it."

Draper's mouth fell open, and then he ran his hands through his black hair – a thing he did when his brains scrambled, and he needed to rethink his process. "Wow. I guess I didn't think of it like that. I, um. Hold on. I'll go get the guys."

Draper was beloved among the workers. He had a caddish smile, the experience of both a pimp and a businessman, and the grace of a prince. No sooner had he told them my reasons for eating in the center of the square did forty men take up their chairs and drag them over to form a half-circle around the platform I was leaning against. The wood at my back was rough, but I liked the stiffness and the slight scratch that didn't bother being tender to my spine. A flock of sparrows alighted on the platform behind me, nudging as close as they possibly could so they could chirp greetings and encouragements in my ear.

Several men offered me their chairs when they came over, but I waved them all off with gratitude and kept to the dirt where I felt I belonged. Draper sat on the step at my left, and Montel took the spot on my right – the two gargoyles fielding the questions that flew at me by the dozens, as they did every night.

Only tonight, the entire square started gathering around me, seeing this as their opportunity to ask all the things they'd been wondering about me – the new girl in town. They started shouting out questions about Common, wondering about small things and important ones in equal measure. The factions disappeared with the simple act of me facing my grief by sitting at the foot of the stage. It was kind of amazing.

"Do all women sit in the dirt up there?"

"No, just the awesome ones."

"What's the schooling like?"

That one was followed by a basic breakdown of the educational system I was most familiar with.

"Does everyone sleep, like you? Or do they not have to use as much magic?"

On and on the questions went until one made my spine stiffen. "Who broke off the engagement? Was it you who left Madigan the Formidable, or the Untouchable who shamed you?"

Draper fielded that one while I tried to scrape my chin

up off the ground. I noticed all of the women looking away, as if the mention of me being jilted by Madigan was something that reflected poorly on me. I didn't understand it, but let them have their strange customs all the same. As I mulled this over, I realized none of the women had spoken to me since word of my broken engagement had spread. They weren't cruel, just treated me as if I wasn't there.

Usually it was just the people gathered around the Province 9 pole, but tonight all the men got their chance to get their interview questions answered, even the uncomfortable ones. I was beyond exhausted, but I didn't care. The regions were finally doing something together, aside from building a wall to keep Morgan out. The lantern light flickered on the faces of the men, women and children alike as they all listened with rapt attention to the mundane details they couldn't get enough of.

Two hours passed, and my head found its way to Draper's knee. His position on the step above me made his leg the perfect pillow. His fingers ruffled the curls that had fallen loose from my ponytail. My hair had been a rich brown when the morning started, but now I'm sure it matched the lighter dust of the road. "Time to turn in, kiddo. Let's get on home." He hoisted me up, steadied me with his arm around my shoulders, and held up his free hand to the people, who didn't bother to hide their "Aw, man!" responses that I had to end Q&A time for the night. "She'll be back tomorrow to talk to you all." Draper smiled when he looked out at the intermingling of the provinces.

"Everyone look to your right and to your left. Greet your new neighbor with a kiss on the cheek. You've all traveled a long way, and could use a friendly face." He squeezed my hand for me to take the wheel, but my verbal well came up empty. I wanted to find my personality and speak to the people, but my face remained unchanged and impassive, my mouth shut.

Draper took over for me. "No matter where we all came from, we're one province now. Love the people who came to you from other places. Honor the long road that brought them here, and be grateful when they honor yours. We're family now, and families eat together at the table. My sister and I will see you all out here tomorrow night."

There was no easy way through the crowd, so Montel flagged one of the dudes who'd worked with us on the wall, Orval. He was stocky, had copper hair, and a get-off-my-lawn attitude that made him the ideal worker, since he had few friends and just wanted to get the job done. Orval and Montel acted as sentries for Draper and me, moving without incident through the crowd that parted at their bodyguard-like stances.

I wish nothing made me think of Link and Mad, but that sure did. I'd depended on my ex-guy's two besties to have my back in crowds like this. They were gone now, and I tried not to feel the sting of the gaping hole they'd left in my heart.

I glanced down at my wrist, frowning at the black

script tattoo that was supposed to offer me protection, to be the Untouchables' signature that kept all the bad things away from me. It matched the more obvious one on my neck, and I wished I could erase them both from my skin. I'd been so excited to get inked – my first tattoos. Little did I know my boyfriend had been nursing his hangover in a whorehouse while I'd been getting marked to declare his loyalty to me. Like a dummy, now I was stuck declaring to Avalon for the rest of my time here that I'd had a guy, and now he was gone. The ink felt like a public shaming now, instead of something I'd been proud to wear. I shoved my hands in the pockets of my jeans, feeling stupid at the constant reminder that all three of them had ditched me, and that I'd trusted in a lie.

Draper's arm around my shoulder kept me upright as we walked toward the mansion, but the throngs of people that wanted to see us safely home did nothing to quell my nerves as they pressed in merrily around us. Crowds had never really bothered me before, but lately I was becoming more uncomfortable with a great many things. It seemed a constant tumble of anxiety churned in my gut, making me skittish as I reached over and clung to my brother.

Draper squeezed my shoulder. "Hey, it's alright. They just want to see you. We'll be home in a few minutes." He kissed my temple, much to the audible gushing of the women who relished in each bit of affection the handsome prince lavished on me. Draper was the most eligible bachelor in the land, now that the Untouchables were gone.

The fact that he wasn't embarrassed to be sweet to his sister skyrocketed him to Justin Timberlake level of fandom. I was happy for him, probably, but the largest emotion that resonated through my bones was that I just wanted to be alone.

3

THE DIVERSION

A few evenings of eating together as a united province started to solidify many of the smiles that stretched beyond territory borders. People were starting to become neighbors, laughing together as they shouted out questions at random for me to answer. The women didn't talk to me, though, which I didn't understand. They didn't seem angry at me, just avoiding my gaze, and refusing to speak to me. I wasn't sure what to make of that.

As the night wore on, I grew more and more tired, as these things tended to go. Finally I begged off any more questioning, wanting to just hang out with them instead of being on display. Actually, what I wanted was to go home, but Draper was having too good a time. I didn't want to ruin his fun just because I wasn't a people person these days.

Draper patted my shoulders after about three minutes of shooting the breeze with a few of the women who ventured near me. "Let's call it early tonight. Dad would be thrilled if you came home and washed up before court. Let's surprise him by bringing you home before you pass out."

I yawned, but was holding my own alright. "Okay. Yeah, he'd like that." Draper helped me to stand, both of us turning when we caught wind of an argument that started to escalate not too far from where we stood. Even my ravens that had been circling overhead noticed the disturbance. Shouting turned to shoving, and others joined in the growing fight. Pretty soon, over a dozen men were throwing punches. "Stop that!" I shouted, indignant that people could act like jackholes after having such a kumbaya kind of night together.

The brawling grew, and pretty soon I found myself too near the fight that I still knew nothing about. Draper ripped two men apart, with Montel and Orval taking his lead and barreling through the jags without apology. Still, there was chaos, and the disquiet only grew from there. My ravens cheeped angrily at the men, and then cried out in unintelligible panic when a second unkindness of ravens flew in from the west to join them. One of the newcomers dropped out of the sky and landed somewhere behind me, but I was too turned around by the fight to locate him on the ground.

My heart seemed to stop beating when a beefy arm

wrapped in a black cloak coiled around my neck from behind. "Stay very still," the low voice warned. When he spoke, I heard the sound of wings flapping and something metallic, coming from the direction of his mouth. "I don't want to bleed ye out here. Too many witnesses." I clawed at the arm as it tightened around my throat, choking me without mercy.

I'd been choked in this very place by Madigan, who'd been mind-controlled by a hooded man in a black cloak. Fear lit me from the inside, and I bucked against him, feeling the bite of his blade slice across the back of my hip. I tried to scream, but I couldn't get a sound out – so firm was his hold on me. I dragged my heels in the dirt as he started to haul me backwards, toward the outer edge of the Town Square, and away from the light. I tried to reach up and gouge at his eyes, but he was too tall for me to get at his face.

His skin smelled like old makeup, and his breath stank like rotting fish. "I could stick ye right here and let ye bleed out in front of your brother, but I won't. I just want ye to know tha I can. I've got big plans for ye, little flower. Your life is mine, and at any moment, I might come to collect it. Sluaghs always collect what's owed them." He spat over my shoulder in disgust, his voice low and laced with a gravelly cadence to it. "Disgrace to the throne, both ye and the prince. Sitting in the dirt like peasants."

I reached up and tried to claw at his eyes again, but the stupid hood was blocking my clumsy fingers. When the knife scraped over my hip again, I thought the scream that filled my ears was my own, but luckily, it was from one of the villagers who'd caught sight of me being dragged away from the fray. "The princess! Someone's grabbed the Avalon Rose! Help!"

A fierce affection rose in me as a group of nearby villagers ran toward me, fearing nothing as they charged the armed man without swords of their own to attack with.

Draper bolted through the crowd, attuned to the sound of my name. He knocked anyone in his path out of the way when he realized with horror the goal of the fight that had started seemingly out of nowhere. The brawl was the diversion. I was the target.

He rushed the man, joining the people who wouldn't let me be taken away in the dark of night. "Sleep well tonight, Princess," the hooded figure snarled in my ear before he let go of me. Then he quite literally vanished into thin air before I could catch sight of his face, leaving only the stench of his breath behind.

4

I GET ALL THE CHICKENS

Security around the mansion was tightened, and a search was sent out through the province to see if anyone could find... a faceless man in a hood who was jonesing to shiv me. If you can believe it, the search didn't turn up any promising leads.

The slice on my hip was treated and bandaged by Jean-Luc, but other than my anxiety growing tenfold, nothing much changed. Urien ordered that I not be out after dark anymore, which I couldn't argue with. We stuck closer to each other after that, him peeking in on me when I was sleeping, and me sneaking out of my room at night to make sure he and Draper were safe and sound.

I returned to the wall two days later, after much debate. Work was pretty much the same, and the days passed without event, though the men were more protective of me on the job. The hard labor gave my hands purpose and helped me calm myself down in the few weeks that followed my attack. I was supposed to go straight home by midnight, which was when my dad held court. I usually adhered to the rules of the house, obeying instead of carving my own path. I had no need to find my own way anymore. I needed the hole in my chest to fill itself, and hoped manual labor and usefulness might do the trick.

The sun had been a little too ambitious that day, beating down on us while we worked tirelessly on the wall. I stayed long after Draper and most of the men threw in the towel to go into town for their supper. I wasn't hungry, but rather addicted to the work. The people had been nothing but great, especially after the attack, but an unease had fallen over me in the past few weeks, making me wary of crowds. Not sure where I got that from. Perhaps the hooded cloak dude.

I went back to the castle long after night fell, hours after Pascal called it a day. Montel and I were the only two left, and I knew he was only staying because Draper had wanted to eat his supper in the Town Square, and I was Montel's unofficial charge.

He walked me back to the mansion, both of us too tired for conversation. I liked Montel for that very reason. I knew next to nothing about him, and he didn't ask questions about me. Montel was a good guy in my books on that shining quality alone. He was tall and lean, but could lift bricks with the best of them. His coffee-colored skin made me ache for Reyn, and by proxy, Lane.

Montel stopped dead in his tracks when the overlarge double front doors opened, and we were greeted by a frown I had not been expecting. "Oh. Hey, Dad. What's up?" We had servants who answered doors. My dad didn't usually do that.

Urien had been announced to the province as being very much alive and back from the twenty-one-year-long coma my mother had put him in. Morgan le Fae was a curse word in our home now. My dad, Draper and I had spent our evenings together getting to know each other both during and after we held court, and had gotten along really well.

Until tonight, I'm guessing.

Urien tapped his foot impatiently on the floor of the grand entryway. "'What's up?' What's up is that you've been out all day. You were supposed to come home when my son did, but I can see Kerdik's warnings, my request, and the reminder of the proper time for court fell on deaf ears."

I leaned in and cupped my ear. "Huh? I can't hear you." I managed a chuckle (but not a smile). "That's a little taste of the hilarity that's in store for you this evening."

Dad shot me a withering look. "I can hardly contain my excitement."

I thought it was precious that Urien had taken to calling Draper his son, even though Draper was technically his nephew. The prodigal thirty-something had been cast out by his own father, Duke Henri, and then adopted by Lane, who had been a mother to me, but was actually my aunt. For all intents and purposes, Draper was my adopted brother, Lane was my mother of choice, and Urien was my dad. Though Urien and Lane weren't together by any stretch of the imagination, Draper and I were without question their children. We were ripe for talk show fodder, but I didn't care. They were my family, and wonky as we were, somehow we worked.

Urien's gaze flitted to Montel, who was on his knees in supplication. "You there. Do you work on the border with my daughter?"

Montel kept his head bowed, his short black hair hiding none of his reverence for the throne. "Yes, your majesty. May it please you, your grace."

"If she goes back out tomorrow, see to it she's sent home with Prince Draper, and not a minute later. Her curfew is midnight, not an hour after."

"Yes, your highness. Begging your forgiveness, my king."

"That's not necessary." Urien frowned, his eyes cutting back to me. "They weren't so frightful in my day."

I moved up the steps, leaned up and pecked my dad's cheek. "This *is* your day. Never forget that." I waved over my shoulder at Montel, who was too afraid to get up off his knees. "See you tomorrow, dude." I shut the doors behind me, bolting them six times, because that's what I'd been instructed to do to keep the mysterious fish-breathed, hooded bad guy away.

I lugged myself up the steps, where two handmaidens were waiting for me with anxious looks on their faces. "Oh, right. Sorry I was late coming home."

"His majesty most high postponed court for you, so we must be quick, your grace," the girl named Aimee warned. Though she was easily five years younger than me, she knew the ropes of castle life better than I did, so I adhered to her rule when I could. I'd insisted when I first moved in that I didn't need handmaidens, but Urien overruled me as soon as he'd reclaimed the throne.

"I can really bathe myself," I insisted, the same way I had every night before for weeks now, but just as before, they insisted it would be faster if they did it, which it kind of was. Their quick movements made me nervous, but it seemed lately everything did. That's why I loved working on the wall. It was predictable, and Pascal left no choice in what was to be done.

In no time at all, I was shoved with gentle hands into a dress and trussed up with my damp curls pinned back in a flattering way I would never have been able to figure out myself. I was more the ponytail-and-go type of girl.

They led me down the stairs and ushered me inside, where I sat on a legit throne next to my dad, with Draper in a throne of his own on Urien's other side. "It's good you could make it, Rosalie," Urien said without a hint of sarcasm. I'd shown up late, and still he was good to me. I couldn't have felt worse.

"Sorry, Dad. I got distracted and forgot the time at work. I'm here now. How can I help?"

"Just be your wonderful self and listen to the people. Seeing you with me is a comfort to them all. Sometimes I wonder if they don't make up problems just to have a reason to come and gaze upon your lovely face."

I yawned through my blush. "You should write poetry. That was super way beautiful. Thank you."

Urien motioned for Herald, who stood at attention at the double doors, to open them and usher the first person inside. A sweaty-faced farmer named Tavin greeted us, and he was squabbling with his neighbor Ramond over territory lines, and how much he should be compensated for his neighbor's two-headed pit bull eating one of his loose chickens.

My dad was fair, listening all the way through before speaking his mind. "Since you cannot agree, the territory shall be split so that each of you has the exact same amount of land. If you find that not to your liking, there are plenty of available plots you can move to, either of you. As for the chicken, your dog should see a leash, and you should know better than to trust your chickens running about with a dog next door. It's like you're parading lunch in front of them."

Tavin's eyes darted to me. "Perhaps if the princess could come and reason with the dog, they wouldn't attack anymore."

This wasn't a huge surprise, and Draper was all over it.

"What a splendid idea. We'll take all your chickens and your dogs, the both of you, and house them here in our barns. I'm sure you can protect and feed your households another way. They'll be far happier with Rosie."

I nodded. "Oh, sure. But fair warning, once I take in an animal, I really don't like letting it go." I waved my hand good-naturedly. "Oh, but I'm sure you have other means to support yourselves. You don't need your chickens to survive."

The uncomfortable stammering produced a muttered apology between the two, who agreed to work things out without having to disrupt the castle any further.

The other cases were much the same. Territory disputes, this man slept with this other man's wife, someone needed help finding work, and so on and so forth. The line was forty deep, and by the time we reached the end, my eyes were barely open.

Still I was restless, unable to quell the anxiety that drove me to fiddle with the sleeve of my dress, and check over my shoulder in the room that was completely secured.

5

MISSING BRITNEY SPEARS

Draper stood and helped me up out of my hard-backed throne. "Maybe don't work so hard tomorrow. You're barely upright."

"Lane," I begged. "She's still not back?"

Draper shrugged. "Foreign relations take time. More immigrants are trickling in, though, so she's on the move, for sure. When she finishes up shaking hands with Duke Lot in Province 5, that'll just leave Province 2, and I don't think she's foolish enough to try bending old Duke Henri's ear."

It was an obvious choice that Draper had started calling Urien "Dad" and referred to his biological father by his first name and formal title only.

"I just miss her. I didn't realize she'd be gone this long. It's been like, almost two months." I twisted my fingers nervously. "You're sure she's not in danger? I've got a bad feeling about it."

Draper was patient with me. I'd gone from possessing a decent amount of confidence and humor, to being an anxious, antisocial, frowning workaholic in the past month. "You've got a bad feeling about everything lately. Lane's still trying to secure more allies for when Morgan attacks again. The more she brings home to us, the fewer will be against us when Morgan comes in for seconds. Plus, if we're united, we'll stand taller under an attack. It's not fair to leave the smaller provinces so unprotected."

"Quit making sense. Just let me whine, and then fix all my problems," I pretended to demand. "I mean, is that too much to ask?"

Draper chuckled at my tired expression. "Get some sleep, kiddo." He smiled graciously when my dad kissed his cheek, and I knew that Urien's utter acceptance of him as a son was starting to heal some of the unhealthy wounds Duke Henri had left on my beloved Draper. "Goodnight, Dad. I'll be in the study if you need anything."

"Thank you, Son."

I caught my dad's hand before he left. "Lock the windows on the first floor before you start reading over the history logs. I mean it." My eyes darted around. "Maybe the second floor, too. Yeah, definitely the first and second floors."

Urien and Draper exchanged a resigned look, knowing

that they would have to allow me to be overbearing. It was my right, since I'd been the most recent of the three of us to be attacked.

The mansion was quiet at this time in the evening. We didn't have a huge staff, since there wasn't much we couldn't do ourselves. The dozen household servants usually corralled in the prep room, which was where the laundry was done and folded, the cleaning supplies were stored, and a large wooden table was provided for them to shoot the breeze without worrying about being beheaded if us stuck-up royals felt like putting on a show. Of course, they all were getting used to the fact that we weren't like Morgan le Fae, but at this time of the night, they treasured their privacy, which was fine by me. I decided to skip the usual late-night snack, and head straight to bed, though I knew I wouldn't be able to sleep yet.

My dad caught me on my way to the stairs, and wrapped his arm around my shoulders. "I'm guessing you'd like to end your night without supper again. I'm wondering how many nights in a row you'll think you can sneak that by me?"

"I ate a big meal in the Town Square," I said with feigned innocence.

"Interesting. Your brother didn't see you there."

"Draper's a lousy snitch," I grumbled. We both knew I was avoiding social interactions where real conversation might happen.

"I wouldn't mind sitting with you while you ate. You can tell me all about your day."

I leaned against the stone wall next to the staircase, my eyes closing for a brief moment while I tried to sum up the boring task that took all of two seconds to describe. "It was the same as yesterday. Just building the wall. I decided to skip answering fifty million questions over stew in the Town Square."

"You didn't eat the villagers' stew tonight. Nor last night."

"Wasn't hungry."

"I assume you're ravenous now, then. Come to the kitchen. Let your father make you something to eat."

Darn his good politics. He knew I wouldn't turn up my nose at his kindness. "Sure. Thanks, Dad."

Urien led me to the deserted kitchen and started assembling a plate of fruit and cheese. "Tell me about your work today."

"I hauled bricks from Point A to Point B. That's pretty much it."

Urien frowned. "Hauling bricks? Draper told me you were supposed to be mixing the mortar with him."

I shrugged. "There was an opening for brick moving, so I jumped on it. Total body workout. I'll be lifting whole houses in no time with my beastly muscles."

"I have no doubt." He shook his head at me. "You didn't have any interesting conversations? Nothing of note happened while you were working?"

"Not really. I mean, there was a brick lifting contest during lunch. I didn't win, if you can believe it. That was all Orval, so if you're looking for a Province 9 strong man, he's your guy."

"The men were respectful to you?"

"Oh, yeah. The ones building the wall are all dudes who want good things for the province. They leave me alone and let me work with them, no problem. They're good guys."

There were a few beats of silence I didn't have the oomph to fill, so I let them hang between us while I ate my dinner as if it was my job. Urien sighed sadly. "You were happier to talk to me when you were Britney Spears. I'm not sure how to get you back."

"I'm here. This is Work-Mode Rosie." I don't know why I was so quiet lately. He was right; I didn't much feel like conversation with anyone. "It's not you," I admitted. "I'm in a funk. I'll defunkify when it passes."

"Are you often in funks like this?" he asked tentatively, choosing his words with care. "It pains me that I don't know you well enough to have that information to pull from. I don't know if this is normal for you or not."

Even my worst funks usually only lasted a day or two. Something in me felt missing, and I just didn't have my usual bouncing back moxie I needed so desperately. "I wouldn't worry. Maybe it's not a funk at all. Maybe this is the new me." I wanted to say that with pride, but the truth of that possibility slammed into me like a punch.

I moved to the sink and washed my mostly empty dish. "Kerdik gone to his fabulous meadow again? I haven't seen him in days."

"Kerdik comes and goes as he pleases. I can ask him to come home, if you like."

"Like you said, he can come and go as he pleases. I won't chain him here."

"Kerdik would like nothing more than if you did exactly that, you know," Urien said by way of a warning.

"He'll come back when he feels like it. Can't blame a guy for not wanting to hang with me morning, noon and night." I wasn't exactly a barrel of laughs anymore. I yawned yet again, just barely covering my mouth.

Urien moved next to me and kissed my forehead. "You look exhausted. Why don't you get some sleep? I'll send up a tray of food for you, in case you'd like more to eat in the night. Perhaps the macarons you're so fond of?"

"Okay."

"Rosalie?"

"Yeah, Dad?"

"I want you home earlier tomorrow. This isn't healthy."

I nodded, guessing arguing would be pointless. "I'm sorry I stayed so late. I won't push myself so hard tomorrow."

He nodded, taking in my slumped demeanor with a scrutinizing eye. "I know you'll push yourself until you feel you've been punished enough. Though why you think you're the one in need of the belt, I'll never know."

I rested my forehead on his sturdy shoulder, inhaling his scent of peppermint oil that I knew I'd never get tired of. "Everything feels upside-down. I'm just glad you're upright. It'll all set itself on a forward course again. Just might take a while."

"Anything I can do?"

"You being you helps." I sighed contentedly when his arm wrapped around the middle of my back in a half hug I wholly needed.

"Talk to me, sweet girl."

I bit my lip through my resistance, and eked out a few things he probably already knew, just to be a team player. "I'm having a hard time sleeping, but I know I need to. The birds are always talking to me, and I'm more tired every morning. I thought if I exhausted myself with work today, that might help me sleep more soundly."

"It's a good theory."

"I should probably turn in."

Urien sighed at my distant demeanor that had become the norm. "Goodnight, dear. I hope to see you tomorrow night. I do look forward to our time together."

I pulled away when the anxiety in my gut spiked again for no good reason. I looked over my shoulder, but nothing was there. "Me, too. Goodnight, Dad. Lock your bedroom door, okay?"

"Of course," he conceded with a sad smile.

Every time I called him my dad, he pressed his palm

over his heart, and looked at me like I was the sun and moon. I felt doubly disappointed in myself for putting in a sucky effort during our time together. My feet dragged themselves up the steps to the quiet of my bedroom, where I checked the locks four times before turning in.

6

DREAM GIRL

There wasn't enough soap in the world for how disgusting I felt the next evening after work, even after I'd been bathed by Aimee. There had been dirt and mortar caked into every square inch of me, and she'd managed to get off maybe eighty percent of it in the limited time she'd been given. The filth was stubborn as it clung to my skin, but after the third bath, I was finally clean enough to wear pajamas.

Only I didn't gravitate to pajamas. There was only one thing I wanted to wear to seal my depression, and it hadn't been washed in over a month. The housekeepers had offered to, of course, but I didn't want to admit that I couldn't bear them washing Bastien's scent away from his red and blue flannel shirt. He smelled like Christmas and cinnamon, and after the hell this month without him had been, the scent was heavenly and indulgent. His oversized shirt fit me like a nightgown, hanging to my knees and sloping off my shoulder. I loved the feel of his shirt shifting around me, and pathetic as it was, I pretended he'd meant to leave the shirt for me, instead of me "forgetting" to pack it with his things before I sent him off to man-in-the-woods rehab.

I'd made more of an effort tonight after court to participate in conversation with my dad and Draper, but we all knew it was a bad act. I begged off the second I counted thirty sentences of normal interaction I'd offered up to convince them that I was fine.

The tray of food the servant brought me at my dad's insistence that I was getting too thin sat on the table in my bedroom. It was probably delicious, and I knew my stomach was hungry after the whole day of manual labor, but my heart wasn't in anything these days. I ate like it was my job and punched out as soon as my stomach was filled enough that it wouldn't be annoying to me.

I collapsed on the bed, which felt like a desert of too much space with just me in the king-sized monstrosity. I didn't even have Abraham Lincoln with me anymore to cozy up with and make me believe that I was a good mother. I don't know why, after over two decades of taking in animals who would eventually split, it still hurt enough to make me feel the constant pang of loneliness. I was usually better at feeling the sadness and moving on.

I'd let my bear baby get stabbed. I'd watched with horror while Madigan ran him through. Possessed as my

Lucky Charms fiancé was, I hadn't been able to save my baby from a bloody and public death. My brave Hamish's head had been crushed under Mad's boot, and I'd been impotent to save them. Tears welled in my eyes, and I pretended they were all and only for Abraham Lincoln and Hamish, though admittedly, a few were for Link, Madigan, Lane, Demi and even Roland.

I pulled on a pair of clean jeans when it dawned on me that I hadn't double-checked that Dad had shut all the windows on the first and second floors. I padded down the steps and moved like a zombie through the rooms and down winding hallways, closing the occasional opened window.

As much as I hated to admit it, I missed Lane with a childish panic. I needed my mom, and might never stop. She'd been my best girlfriend my whole life, and now that I barely recognized my life, I wanted her there to be my touchstone while Avalon rocked me around without mercy.

I made it halfway through the second floor of the house before the ground started to tip. I stumbled through the hall and tumbled into the next room to check the windows there, my body protesting how long I would be allowed to exhaust it. The small room with green and silver furniture and draperies had plenty of places to lounge around, but I couldn't make it to any of them. I collapsed on the enormous oval-shaped emerald rug, deciding that would be as good a place as any to make a bed. My head was too heavy to hold up anymore, so I laid it on the rough fabric, my eyelids shutting without my full consent.

~

"WHAT DO YOU THINK YOU'RE DOING?" KERDIK ASKED FROM behind me.

I'm not sure how long I'd slept, but when my head rose and swam in protest, I knew it wasn't long enough. I glanced around the room, unsure where I was at first. I blinked into focus one of the house's many adorned studies. It looked like a decorator from the Victorian era had been given a blank check. This one had an emerald chaise in the corner next to a bookshelf that wouldn't dare collect dust. I so wanted to know what each book said. The silver frames on the walls held portraits of scenery so pretty, I wanted to roll around in the green of it all, but was too depressed to commit to the effort. "Just making sure the house is secure. Someone could sneak in through a window," I said, rubbing my eyes.

"And you just decided to sleep on the floor?" He called down the hallway. "I found her!"

Kerdik eyed my bedraggled and confused state with a pensive look on his face. He pursed his lips before going over my head and rescuing me from myself. "That's enough worry and work out of you for one night. You simply must learn how to enjoy life with a house full of servants. They can tend to the windows. To bed with you, darling." He moved forward and scooped me up in his arms, ignoring my weak protest as he carried me up the stairs like a damsel.

"But it's dangerous! I have to make sure the windows are latched. My dad! Is he alright? I need to check on him."

"Urien's absolutely fine, though we've all gone a bit insane searching for you. It's only due to my blood in your tattoo that I was able to find you in this massive place. You've got to stop worrying about every little thing. This isn't like you."

When I heard my dad's voice boom out my name as he trotted up the steps to meet us, I burst into embarrassing tears. "I thought you were dead!"

Urien stopped short, his hand on his heart. "Why would you think that? You saw me whole and well when we held court this evening, and our chat afterwards. Do I not look well? I can call Jean-Luc back to the palace if you're worried. He can give me a look." He glanced down at his white dress shirt and gray trousers, curious as to what had led me to this conclusion. Remy was off with Lane, and Jean-Luc had been setting up an office in the province with several other healers to provide healthcare to everyone. I hadn't seen him since the cloaked fish-breath dude sliced a line across the back of my hip, and he'd stitched me up.

"Lane's gone! Everyone keeps leaving, but you stayed. I know someone's going to take you away from me!" I sniveled, knowing I was irrational and a little unhinged. "I told you to close the windows! Someone could sneak in and kill you. I told you how dangerous the windows are!"

Urien, to his credit, handled my crazy with grace and kindness to rival any saint. His voice was deep, and seemed to coo around my heart, wrapping me with his warmth that never seemed to run out. "Darling, you worry about so many things now. You can't go wandering about like this. You need sleep. I assure you, everyone is quite safe."

I wanted to argue that Demi had died in a palace easily enough, but I wasn't exactly coherent. I sobbed into Kerdik's crisp white shirt instead while he cradled me in his arms. You know, like a respectable adult. I barely recognized myself. Beneath my unrest and panic, I was ashamed of my behavior.

"I'll watch her for the night. I'm back for another day at least now. You go back to your studies. There's much to read up on, old friend." Kerdik didn't wait for a response, but moved up the steps with me in his arms, He had the fixed, graceful movements any ice skater would envy.

He used his elemental magic to make my wood door swing open, and then carefully set me down on the large bed. He kissed my cheek, taking in my swaying state with a frown. "You're alright to dress for bed by yourself?"

"I should go check on Draper." Dread dawned on me afresh as I stumbled toward the door. "Oh my goodness! I didn't make sure the window down the hall from his bedroom was bolted! Draper!" My heart started pounding, fearing something terrible had happened to my brother.

Kerdik captured me in his embrace before I reached the door. His arms around me were strong, and his voice was slow and steady. "Love, your brother's absolutely fine. Stay in your room and get ready for bed." He walked me over to the bed and sat me down again. Then he leaned me forward, resting my forehead to his navel. "I'm worried about you."

"I'm worried about my family. Can you go check on them for me?"

He looked down on me with a clouded gaze and a frown tugging down the corners of his mouth. "Of course, if that's what you wish."

I was grateful for the privacy when he let himself out, promising to be back in a while with some hot tea. I clumsily kicked off my jeans and crawled under the rose-colored comforter, hoping a deep sleep would claim me.

7

ROSIE, THE IRRATIONAL LUNATIC

I tossed in the giant bed, crying into the sleeve that was far too big for my arm. The owner of the flannel shirt wasn't there to hold me. Even though I'd lived most of my life without him, the lack of his added protection felt like being left naked and exposed to life's cruelties, with no backup.

I missed Judah, who had slept by my side for so many years. I despised the months we had to be apart, pretending like it was totally normal to live without the functioning wheels on our bicycle built for two. There was a Judah-shaped hole in my heart to match the others left by the friends and family I'd made in Avalon who hadn't been able to stick around.

I fell into a short, fitful sleep, and then woke in the night to a bolt of anxiety. I hadn't heard anything about

Draper or Urien, and worried a burglar had broken into the house. I got out of the bed, telling myself I was just going to check on them, as I had for so many nights in a row now. My feet dragged on the way to the door after I lit the lantern, but I jumped in surprise when Kerdik's form filled my hazy vision in the hallway. He moved toward me and leaned against the frame when I opened the door half-way. My face drained of color. "Is everyone alright?" Grief shot through me, unbidden. "He's dead, isn't he!"

Kerdik's eyes widened. "Who's dead?"

"My dad! I closed my eyes for two seconds, and someone snuck in through the window and killed him!" I covered my mouth as the scene played out in my fractured imagination. "It's all my fault! I didn't check the window on the first floor four doors down from Draper's bedroom!"

Kerdik was holding an empty teacup and saucer in his hand. He studied my face far too closely before responding. "Urien's perfectly fine. I just spoke with him down in his study before I came up here to watch you toss and turn. You've nothing to worry about."

"Draper?" I asked, scared all over again.

"He's fine, as well." He shook his head at me. "You look like you haven't slept in ages. I know you're long overdue. You used to be you. Where did you go?"

I wiped my tears on my damp flannel sleeve, trying to compose myself and recall my personality. "Oh, you with the compliments."

"You know what I mean. Your insides used to be so bright that they shone through and lifted everything around you. And forgive me, but tears and irrational fear add nothing to a woman's beauty."

I looked down at the oversized flannel shirt that wasn't even mine, taking in just how pathetic I'd become. I didn't know who I was anymore. I'd lost some vital part of me that made me act like a loon who lost her mind over an imagined break-in. I sniffed and swiped at my eyes with my baggy sleeve. "I know what you're thinking: it doesn't get much sexier than this." I motioned to the old shirt and my hair that had dried in funky waves hours ago.

"That's exactly what I was thinking, actually." Kerdik pushed the door open the rest of the way and then locked it behind him after moving into the bedroom. He let out a weighted sigh when I fastened the other three locks, just in case. "I can't look at you in that shirt anymore. It's depressing, and it's starting to smell."

"I like sleeping in his shirt," I admitted the obvious, owning up to the pitiful nature of the beast.

Kerdik shook his head at me, taking the lantern from my hand and hanging it on the hook near the door. "Young love. I remember now why I don't bother with it anymore. Go on behind your partition and take that thing off. I'm serious. I can't look at you in his clothes another second."

I hugged myself, that nagging anxiety making me antsy as I shifted from foot to foot. "It makes me feel safe."

"Darling, you are safe. I'm here." A tender expression crossed his features, and he slowly began to unbutton his charcoal vest. "You can wear mine instead."

My gaze climbed up to his face, perplexed. "But you like your shirts unwrinkled."

"I like *you* unwrinkled, and if you don't sleep, there won't be any undoing that. Run and change, now. We haven't got all night."

I didn't know what to do when Kerdik put his shirt in my hand. He was rarely without long sleeves, and I could tell by the way he kept running his hands down his bare arms that he didn't like how on display his green skin was. He wore his undershirt, but the lack of long sleeves I could tell was a big step for him. The dim light of the lantern flickered, making his muscular arms seem to glow with a Wicked Witch of the West kind of aura. Only he wasn't a wicked witch – at least not to me. He was my friend, and no matter how many times I pushed him away with my crazy lately, he kept coming back to see if I'd returned myself to us. "You're being sweet to me," I noted, gazing up at him in confusion. "I'm being an irrational lunatic, and you're being nice. When did we switch roles?"

"Yes, you are a lunatic. Though I've been quite unbalanced toward you on a far worse scale in the past, so hopefully this tips us more toward even footing. Would you like me to send a servant to fetch Jean-Luc? It's been a while since he's given you a look."

"No, I'm fine. And you don't have to think about the time you froze me in the tub. I know you're working on controlling your temper these days. I can see it. You let me rub scrambled eggs on your face last week, and the house only shook a little. Progress."

"That was a month ago, not last week." He rolled his eyes at me. "Just take the shirt."

I moved behind the partition and changed out of the dirty rag I'd been using as basically a wearable blankie. Totally pathetic. I splashed a little water on my face from the basin on the stand and buttoned Kerdik's white shirt up over my underwear. The crisp material was far more breathable against my skin, and made me feel like I was gloriously naked, though the shirt fell to the middle of my thigh. Bastien was just plain bulkier than Kerdik, and it showed in the fit of each man's clothing on my curvy form.

I came out from behind the partition, the lantern's light dancing on my bare legs. "Thanks, K. I think maybe I needed someone to take his shirt away. Now he can really be gone." I pushed the sleeves up my arms. "After tonight, I'll sleep in regular nightgowns. Thanks for getting me over the hump. You're a good friend. I know I'm being a loser about everything lately. I can't seem to shake myself out of it."

Kerdik swallowed thickly, his gaze lingering on my form. "No trouble at all. I rather like the look of you in my clothes." He stepped toward me and unbuttoned the cuffs, then took his time folding them over and over, so that they hung to my elbows at an even length on both arms. "Much better." He eyed the top button that he always kept fastened, but I had left undone.

"Thank you. The super long sleeves do get annoying in the night."

"Let me be good to you." He tucked a lock of my unruly hair behind my ear so I couldn't hide from him. "It worries me to see you so troubled. I don't do worry."

I wrapped my arms around my middle, feeling low enough to admit aloud what I needed. I couldn't look at him; what I wanted was too embarrassing. "Will you stay with me? Just until I fall asleep?"

Something shifted between us, though I couldn't put my finger on just what. He tipped my face up to his, so he could take in the full scope of just how much that request had cost my pride. "You know I'll stay with you forever. You only had to ask."

He took my hand and led me to the bed, backing into it until he was sitting on the mattress. He pulled me to stand between his long legs, his hands still holding mine, like he was wary to let that small contact go. He glanced down at his bare arms with a self-conscious frown. I let go of his hands and traced my way up his forearms, rubbing the muscles, regardless of whether or not he was capable of getting sore. "I never get to see your skin much. Why is that?"

A wind belted through the room out of nowhere,

knocking the window open with a bang. I jumped and stumbled over to latch it shut. I leaned out slightly to grab hold of the window, but the edge was just out of reach. I felt Kerdik's hand on the back of my hip, knowing exactly how to touch me. He moved me aside and leaned out to shut it for me with his much longer arms. "No, no," he breathed when he turned around. "That shirt is completely transparent on you. I don't want anyone seeing your body out there."

I glanced down in the dim lantern's light. "Oh, yikes. Thanks. Was the comment about your skin an off-limits topic or something? I didn't mean to make you upset by it. I like your skin, but you act like it's something to hide."

"It is something to hide. It's bright green, or haven't you noticed?"

I eyed his sour expression and reached out to make what was probably the wrong move. With slow and clumsy fingers, I untucked his undershirt, maintaining eye contact as my hands trilled across his bare abdomen. He stopped breathing, but lifted his arms when I tugged his shirt over his head, revealing a leonine and sculpted purely green torso. His arms made to cover his chest and stomach, but I brushed away his effort. "Beautiful," I whispered, astonished at how amazing a man could look when dowsed in a pure color that held no apologies. I didn't hesitate to reach out and stroke the ripples in his abdomen. My finger circled his navel, as if I had the right to do what I wanted with his body. "I wonder why the hair's darker here," I mused, running my nails through the thin tuft that trailed from his belly button downward and disappeared beneath the waistline of his chocolate-colored trousers. "I thought it'd be blue."

Kerdik moistened his lips as his breathing picked up, his light green eyes climbing up my body to meet my gaze. "You are trouble. Nothing but trouble when you've got no filter like this."

When my fingers stroked down his naked side, goosebumps broke out on his flesh, and I appreciated his glorious skin anew. I didn't know who I was anymore, but the green had a conviction about it that fascinated me. The green knew exactly what color it was, and didn't permit any amount of confusion. I longed for such certainty. I'd been the ugly girl, the lost girl, the rich girl, the stupid girl, and now? Now I just felt broken. "Do you think I could…" I wanted to be closer to something so magnificent and sure. My fingernails trilled over his chest, alighting on sensitive parts that made him shiver.

Kerdik bit down on his lips before his gaze tightened. "Okay, you're going to sleep right now."

"Maybe I already am asleep." The line between sleep and waking was so blurred in my mind now, that sometimes in the night I couldn't tell the difference. "Maybe you're a dream."

His voice was quiet when he leaned in, brushing his cheek to mine. "Am I a good dream?"

I wobbled when I leaned up on my toes, holding onto

his biceps to steady myself so I didn't fall over. "A shirtless dream is always a good one."

A low rumble vibrated from Kerdik's chest, and his hands wrapped around me to squeeze my waist possessively. "Don't be their princess; only be my queen." His fingers brushed across the swell of my backside, giving us both the green light and the red at the same time, as we pivoted on the edge of our strange friendship. "You have no idea what you're saying, and I'm all too aware of it. I have half a mind to tear my shirt clean off you and suck on these plump breasts. They've been teasing me for far too long." He shook his head.

"All talk." I smiled at the seduction of a chase neither of us had a right to be in.

"I think you should probably tell me to leave." When I didn't say anything, Kerdik's fingers started to trace my throat, gravitating toward the needy whine that escaped my lips. "You've left your whole neck exposed here; you know what that does to me."

"Kerdik, I..." When his lips caressed my neck, any reason left in my brain turned into a gratuitous moan. His mouth opened to suck on my skin, tasting the juncture between my shoulder and my neck as if I was utterly lickable. His arms went around my waist, jerking me to his front so that our pelvises kept no secrets from each other.

"We can't do this," he scolded himself. He popped open one of the buttons on my borrowed shirt, his fingers dexterous and capable. Sirens went off in my head when another button came undone and the collar slid over my shoulder and down my arm, giving him more real estate to nibble on as his hands clutched me to him. He reached between us and hiked up the hem at my thighs so he could grip the swell of my leg, his fingers squeezing as if to test my ripeness. "Send me away."

I shook my head, but maybe I shouldn't have. Maybe I should've pushed the sexy man in my bedroom far away. Lane would have told me that a woman who didn't know who she was shouldn't be figuring that mystery out with anyone else; she should get herself together first.

I didn't want Kerdik to go, but I knew we probably shouldn't be doing the breathy things we were contemplating. It began to dawn on me that Kerdik was far older and more experienced than I was at the art of seduction. I didn't know the game, so I was pliable under his ministrations, when perhaps I should've been rigid.

But part of me had wanted this from the very start. I didn't have the words to put to it when I first saw him in the storm so very long ago, but the longing was there. No matter how many people warned me away, what had started out as attraction had bloomed into friendship, and was now peaking into a lust I had no reason to deny anymore.

Kerdik's hands were simultaneously rough and gentle, the pressure firm but smooth. "Tell me to leave the province. Tell me your life is better without me by your side."

"You know I'd never say that."

His fingers teased the inside of my thigh, climbing higher as my knees shook with the trepidation of the unknown. I felt him guiding me backwards. Instead of questioning the moment or overthinking a future I was never sure would be there in the morning, I let the lantern's light dictate my pliability. As the flickering flame danced on our skin, so my body moved for Kerdik.

"Lie down," he whispered, his voice low and ragged in my ear. "Your eyes have teased me long enough." It wasn't even an effort for him to lower my form across my bed, my body trembling beneath his.

I finally found my higher brain function, but it didn't come out in time. "Kerdik, wait!" I squeaked as the top of my shirt slid down to a PG-13 level, leaving me exposed enough for my arms to band around my chest, and trapping my sleeves with my elbows.

He looked down on me with affection and longing, as if I was someone precious to him. "Cover yourself as long as you like," he offered, and then leaned down to kiss my cheek. He was careful to keep his lips from mine, so the moment didn't get ruined by the reality that I would breathe fire. White lilies sprang up all around us, blooming from the comforter itself and tickling my bare arms with their delicate petals. He picked one and ran it from my nose, down my throat and danced it along the horizon of my breasts. Maybe that's who I was. Maybe I wasn't broken; maybe I was delicate. He sniffed the flower, and then slowly lowered his nose to my cleavage, burying his face in the valley that was winched shut by the arm I had banded across my chest.

Neither of us were surprised that my back arched, nor that my knees parted. His lips affixed themselves to my sternum, and then kissed a trail of fire-laced lust downward, inching lower until I was panting and writhing beneath his agile body. Kerdik was playing my form as if it was an instrument he needed to stroke to bring out the sweet melody of my strangled cries.

I wanted to feel it all, but suddenly Kerdik wasn't on top of me anymore. I blinked, and raised myself up on my elbows when I found him clear across the room, his back to the wall. His eyes were wide as if *I* was the danger – me, armed with nothing but his shirt and my willingness to let the night take us where it pleased. The lilies around me remained fragrant, but we were separate now, with too much distance between our heated bodies. "We can't do this!" Kerdik chided us both. "For too many reasons, we have to stop now."

While I wanted and wanted, I did my best to put my libido on hold and respect his wishes. "I'm sorry, Kerdik. Was that too much?"

"It's never enough, and that's the problem. We can't... You'll regret all of this in the morning, so I guess I'll have to be the adult tonight." When I made to stand from the mattress, he motioned for me to get under the covers. "Into bed with you, delicious little nymph." His voice turned sharp, as if I was the problem. "And button that shirt!"

I frowned at him, but obeyed. "Oh, fine. You know, usually my dream guys don't mind it when I—"

Kerdik's voice was sharp, and held a note of panic beneath the command. "If you know what's good for you, you'll lay down right now. I've never been known for having great self-control, and you're prancing on the outer edges of mine right now." He lowered me down onto the mattress and pressed a chaste kiss to my lips. "Get some sleep, darling. We can talk in the morning."

"You'll still be here? You're not running off?"

I could practically feel his body beaming at my admission that I wanted him to stay. "If you're here, then that's where I'll be." He retrieved the china cup he'd brought up and turned it over on its saucer. He squeezed his fist a few times, and from nowhere, herbs appeared in his palm and crushed themselves as they fell into the cup. He observed the bags under my eyes as he filled the cup with warm water from his hands. "Drink this, temptress. It'll help you stay asleep. You keep waking every other hour or so. You can't keep going on like this. You'll seduce the wrong man, if you're not careful."

"Are you the wrong man?" I asked, blinking up at him through my daring.

Kerdik didn't answer me, but held my gaze, saying too many things with his eyes. "Drink."

I didn't bother arguing, and downed the cup in one go. Then Kerdik climbed into the bed beside me, sighing contentedly when I curled up like a cat in his arms. I stroked his chest as if it was my plaything, and listened to his breathing start to syncopate.

Kerdik fondled my spine and strummed his fingers across the swell of my butt until my eyelids grew heavy. Finally, I fell asleep without worry that life would be all wrong when I opened my eyes in the morning.

8

THE PROBLEM AND THE SOLUTION

I didn't work quite as manically the next day, or the day after that. It was two whole weeks of me learning to pace myself and deal with the knot that never seemed to go away in my gut. Kerdik and I ate breakfast together in companionable silence every morning after that first night that I slept in his arms, and though I was grateful for his presence, I still felt the ache in my chest at the absence of so many people in my life.

"Not hungry again?" he remarked. "You're whittling down to a stick. I admit, I like the curvier aspects of you."

"I hadn't noticed," I joked. He'd stroked my backside and snuggled my breasts every night for two weeks now in bed while I slept in his shirt. Some of the evenings ended in a bickering fight, but we managed to get along on others. After our one sexy night, we'd tried to keep things PG, and had, for the most part, succeeded. I was anxious and overly exhausted, so I wasn't the most pleasant person to live with these days. No matter how attracted I was to Kerdik, I was in no position to be entertaining sexy thoughts about anyone, broken as I was.

It was when Kerdik commented on it that I realized I was only stirring my oatmeal, and not actually eating much of it. I shoveled in a few bites and took my bowl to the sink. "I'm not trying to be weird. I see how far off the rails I am these days. I don't know why I feel so out of it still. I would've thought having you in bed with me would've helped, but I still tossed and turned."

"You shouldn't be so stubborn about my potions. They're meant to help you."

"I don't want you to have to drug me to sleep. I need to start sleeping without help. I don't know what my deal is."

He motioned for me to come to him, and wrapped his arm around my hips when I stood next to his stool at the kitchen counter. "Be patient with yourself. Give your *lueur* time to settle back into your body. It takes longer for some than for others. Though, I've never known it to take this long."

I slumped against Kerdik, my body molding itself fluidly around his. "He's got my *lueur* still, so that's not it," I sighed, still unable to bring *his* name to my lips. "I'm just in a funk. Funkalicious Rosie, they'll call me. I might even request that it's my work name out on the wall today. It'd make a pretty decent rap name, too, if I ever decide to turn in the crown for a life as a totally dope rap master." I started beatboxing, just because I'm awesome, and frankly, because it usually confused the crap out of Kerdik. I still couldn't smile, but I liked it when other people did.

Kerdik stiffened and pulled back to gape at me. "Please tell me you're making one of your little jokes no one gets. You took your *lueur* back from Bastien before you sent him away, right?"

I wasn't sure if I should feel embarrassed that I hadn't thought to do that. "I mean, he was unconscious. How was I supposed to take it back? I wasn't about to kiss it out of him when he was stone drunk like that."

"How have we not discussed this?!" he shouted out of nowhere. He pinched the bridge of his nose as if my incompetence on how to grow a unicorn from scratch pained him. "If you dismiss your *Guardien*, you have to take your *lueur* back from him, otherwise you're still tied. How did you think you were ever going to get a new *Guardien*?"

I shrugged. "I dunno. No one ever went over all the logistics with me. I wasn't planning on taking another *Guardien*. Too much drama with the last one."

"You need protection!" he bellowed.

"What for? I have you. I watch your back, you watch mine."

Kerdik shot me a simpering expression and crossed his arms over his chest. "That's very cute. You need a *Guardien*, Rosie. Your father and I have already taken applications from dozens of willing men who are eager to take Bastien's place. Urien's been putting it off until you were yourself again, but now I see we would've been waiting forever."

"Huh? What are you talking about? Are you seriously thinking of auctioning me off like Morgan did?"

"Of course not. Not everyone falls in love with their *Guardien*. They're mostly seen as part of the family – a brother or father or son."

My indignation deflated at his logic. "Oh, then I'll hold off on the tirade I was about to spew at you."

"What did you think Urien and I have been doing for the past few days while you were out working on the wall?"

"Mysterious magical stuff? Drinking scotch and talking about getting the hippies off our lawn, like old people do? How should I know? I thought you and Dad were just shooting the breeze, hanging out and catching up."

He shook his head at me. "I swear, it's like you want to get abducted." He threw up his hands, like I was the one being a problem. "Well, now we've got to get Bastien back here. Are you happy with yourself? All that time trying to move on from him, and I have to invite him right back into our home."

I quirked my eyebrow at him, leaning my hip on the counter. "There are about fifteen things wrong with everything you just said. Relax your butthole, K. You're all worked up over a minor hiccup."

The stones started rattling, and I heard a few servants out in the hallway squeak with fear and scurry out of the palace, lest it fall on their heads. My dad and Draper ran into the kitchen, ready to battle whatever needed their reckoning. "What is it? Why's the house shaking?" Urien asked, his brown eyebrows furrowed. He had sporadic streaks of the lightest silver snaking through his hair, making him look distinguished even when he was frazzled.

I rolled my eyes at Kerdik's tantrum. "Kerdik's full of drama this morning."

"Drama? You act like... like..." He spluttered, but was too livid to work out a whole sentence. A few trails of dust fell down from the ceiling between us.

"Bring it all down on your own head, you jag! Bury us all in the rubble because it's just now dawning on you that I wasn't raised here." I ignored the trembling house around me and turned to the newcomers. "He's throwing a fit because I didn't know I was supposed to get my *lueur* back before I sent Hermit Bob away."

Draper smacked his forehead. "Oh! No wonder you haven't been able to calm down. Oh, man. Rosie, why'd you do that?"

"I didn't know I was supposed to take it back! No one told me."

Draper rubbed the nape of his neck, and I could see the past month and a half of my lunacy finally making sense to him. "Okay, kiddo. I'll take care of it. I'll get Bastien back here quick."

"Throwing a fit?" Kerdik raged, his voice shrill. "You haven't begun to see my temper, Rosie!"

At this, a tile fell from the ceiling, landing with a crack between us. Urien and Draper cried out in alarm, but I was just plain pissed. "Would you look what you did? For the record, this is *my* house, not *ours*. You're a guest here, and you best believe you'll be fixing that tile."

"Oh, I 'best believe'? Am I your servant?"

"No, you're the pain in my butt right now. You're dancing on my last nerve, K."

Urien shook his head. "You'll calm yourself around my daughter, Kerdik. Bringing down our home won't get you any peace in the end."

Kerdik let out an angry breath and pressed his hands together under his lips. Finally the house stopped shaking as he reined in his temper. "You're acting like a brat, but at least now I know it's because you're missing your *lueur*. I'll go find Bastien and get it back. Then I'm cramming that thing down your throat before I strangle you!"

"Don't do me any favors!"

He guffawed, ignoring Urien's wary glances and Draper's sniggering at our fight. "Do you hear yourself? Kings and queens sell entire kingdoms for the chance at one of my favors."

"Yes, you're so important. Can you fix a ceiling? Because really that's all I'm asking you to do. If you can't do that, I highly doubt getting an Untouchable back here is within the realm of your abilities." I shook my head. "And I don't want to see him. The only reason I'd need my *lueur* back is if I was taking on a new *Guardien*, which I already told you, I don't need."

Kerdik leveled his finger in my face, his jaw clenched. "You're going to need a string of *Guardiens* to protect you from me if you don't watch it."

"Watch what? This?" I started doing the running man just to piss him off and show him that I wouldn't be intimidated. In hindsight, not my most mature "screw you," but it served its obnoxious purpose.

"Rosie!" Kerdik bellowed in warning, drawing both syllables out.

I touched my fingertip to his and made a patronizing kissing sound. Then I leaned up and pecked his cheek just to piss him off. "I don't need a *Guardien*. I need you to fix my ceiling and stop throwing a fit over every little thing. So my mood's a little off. So what? I caught my boyfriend in a whorehouse. I think a little wallowing is par for the course."

Draper answered before Kerdik could spit out his acerbic retort. "You need your *lueur* back, regardless. No doubt Bastien can feel the anxiety, too. It's part of the magic of the bond between a *Guardien* and his charge. It's painful to be far from each other, makes you both restless. You'll live, but you're going to feel off for the rest of your life until you get it back, or get him here. You feeling this way isn't just because you broke up, and it won't go away in time. It'll only get worse. You're already more neurotic than you were a few weeks ago. Soon enough, you won't be able to sit still. Kerdik's right. You need it back if you're dismissing Bastien."

I let out a heavy sigh. "Okay. Could I not be here for the whole dramatic thing, though? Could you do me a solid, be my big brother and get it from him for me? I'll owe you a favor, for sure. I just really can't face him right now."

"Of course, Ro. Don't think on it another second."

Kerdik threw his arms into the air, exasperated. "That's exactly what I just said I would do for you! How is it Draper says the same thing, and suddenly you're all agreeable?"

"Draper was nice to me. You yelled. I tend to go spontaneously deaf when people yell at me."

Kerdik's teeth ground together as he slammed the flat of his hand down on the counter, making the granite crack clean down the middle. "Oh, you make me crazy!"

I pointed at the wreckage in accusation, my voice shrill. "Would you look at what you just did? Stop breaking my stuff!"

Kerdik jerked his chin at me. "I was just going to fix it. Would you get off my back?" With his elemental energy crap, Kerdik repaired my counter in under five seconds. "There! Are you happy?"

"I'm pretty sure you meant to say, 'I love you, Rosie. I'm sorry I lost my temper and tried to break your house.' I mean, honestly. What's Lane going to say when she gets back?"

"Lane will say, 'Master Kerdik, can I get you some tea?'

'Master Kerdik, whatever you wish shall be done.' That's how normal people talk to me."

I pretended to barf all over his shirt. "Did somebody run off with *your lueur* or something? You're a little more egotistical than usual today."

Kerdik whirled on his heel and barked at my father, "Urien, would you handle your daughter?"

Urien's wide eyes hadn't calmed the entire time. I think he was just now getting a handle on our hard-swinging dynamic. The corners of his mouth started twitching upward, though he tried to hide his amusement. "Darling, perhaps you should go rest while we wait for Bastien to return. Kerdik, old friend, I can't imagine what you hope to accomplish by shouting at my daughter in my presence."

"Fine!" we both yelled. Then I called over my shoulder, "I'm too worked up to sleep, though. I'll be on the wall if anyone needs me." Then to Kerdik, I spouted, "And don't you dare step a toe outside this palace until you clean up the mess you made, young man."

"Sass me again, and I'll turn you over my knee myself!" Kerdik countered, married to his temper and single for life.

I threw him the middle finger before I marched out of the kitchen, chin in the air and anxiety churning in my belly.

9

ROSIE THE FORMIDABLE

I kept to myself for the most part on the job the next few days. My head stayed down as I tried to quell the nerves that churned in my gut. Kerdik and I did our best to stop fighting, but our friendship usually banked on *him* being the unstable one, not both of us. We'd argued so much one of the nights that he'd stormed out and sent Draper to watch me while I slept – or more accurately, while I tossed and turned. I didn't need a mirror to know that I had bags under my eyes and looked like a frazzled version of my former self, but it wasn't as if I was auditioning for any beauty contests. At night when my family held court, Urien and Draper stopped waiting for my labored response on most matters. My mind was too unsettled to be of much use in the academic sense. Besides, my dad liked to rule on the side of unswerving black and white, no matter the heartfelt pleas and dodgy circumstances. Once I understood the laws of the land, I was pretty well trained on how to be useful, should he need a day off.

Pascal assigned me to work mixing mortar, since Kerdik had noticed a long cut across my back from when I'd been lugging bricks the day before. That had been World War III between us, or more realistically, Word War XXVII, since we were at each other's throats more often than not these days. We usually made up by the time I passed out in his arms.

I had sweat running down my back, making my tank top stick to my skin. A few women strolled down the line of men, offering water and rolls they'd just baked.

An older woman with wrinkly fingers laid a roll at my side. "You know," she said to me conspiratorially, "you don't have to work with the men like this. I'll make sure the women don't shun you." It was the first time a woman outside the mansion had spoken to me since it all went south.

My nose crinkled in confusion. "Huh? Why would they shun me?"

"Oh, you know. Because your fiancé left, and shamed you."

I gaped at the gall of this woman, and tried to hurriedly talk myself down from lashing out. "So let me get this straight. If a woman gets dumped, she then has to deal with every other woman being a snob to her? You'd really kick a woman when she's down?"

The old lady blinked at me. "It's how things are done. If a man left, there's clearly something wrong with her."

"Nonsense. If you hear of that happening to any other women in the village, you come straight to me and tell me about it. That's terrible. Band around your sister who's grieving. We should all have some respect for other people's pain." I leveled my gaze at her. "Are there other women in Province 9 who are being shunned like this?"

She nodded carefully, not expecting to step into my wasp nest. "Of course."

"Your official mission from the Avalon Rose is to go home and bake each of them a loaf of bread. Then you'll spend the next week visiting every one of them in their homes, listening as if you give a crap about the women who aren't lucky enough to have kings as fathers." It was beginning to make sense why many of the women didn't look me in the eye anymore during the nighttime suppers, and why none of them spoke to me.

Her mouth fell open, but she recovered quickly. "Yes, your grace."

I watched her scurry off, and tried to stifle the venom in my soul before it rooted too deep for a smile to fend off (should one ever surface again).

"You're going to go home with blisters if you mix that without the gloves," Montel warned me, wiping the sweat that slid from his dark brow.

"Yeah, I know. They keep sliding off me. They're men's

gloves, and my hands are just plain too small. I'll give them another try, though."

"Why don't you take a break? You look about ready to fall over."

"I'm alright. Gotta get this wall built."

Montel chuckled, taking a swig from his canteen. "Pace yourself. It's a large province, and we want the wall to encompass the whole thing. This is years of work, your majesty."

I shook my head, donning the sturdy gray gloves that went up my whole forearm. "I told you to call me Rosie. I'm not exactly ruling a kingdom right now." Even though Aimee had braided my hair into a tight French braid, a few strands always inevitably came loose and stuck to my neck.

Montel sobered. "No, no. I wouldn't dream of disrespecting King Urien by calling his daughter by her first name, like his family is on the same level as me. That he's back? It's a miracle none of us thought we'd see. I won't risk his wrath after waiting for so long to get him back."

"You were from Province 3 before people started merging into 9, but you were still counting your lucky pennies, hoping to get my dad back? He was from Province 1."

"Of course. But Morgan le Fae wasn't always in charge. When King Urien ruled Province 1 with her as an equal, there was harmony in the land. Everyone loved all the rulers, no matter which part of Avalon we came from. It was when Morgan le Fae started taking over that the divisions grew so sharply defined. But those of us who believe that Avalon is worth saving held out hope that one day our king would return, and unite us once again."

"What about the other dude rulers?"

"Oh, some of the dukes are fine. Many of the duchesses were great, as well, back when they were alive. The dukes do what they can with what they've been left. But King Urien loved his people, loved his land. He was much like you in that respect."

I churned the mortar with the giant wood stick, but it didn't feel all that effective with the giant gloves on. "Like me?"

"You're helping rebuild the wall, not just ordering it be done. I have no doubt that once the king is fully back on his feet and the kingdom in order, he'll be down here with the rest of us laborers. Why do you think none of us tire of the work?"

"I thought it was just because you're all awesome."

Montel smirked at me. "That, we are. But it's also because we want to work beside our king once again. Show him we never gave up on Avalon, and that Morgan le Fae didn't break us, either."

I was about to tell Montel how much I appreciated him being so cool to me, but one of my handmaidens from the mansion ran down the path toward me with a giddy expression. Aimee was around seventeen, and seemed nice enough, though I didn't know much about her. Most of the servants gave me a wide berth because they were afraid of

Kerdik. Though she'd seen me naked dozens of times while helping me bathe and dress, she was usually in and out of my bedroom in twenty minutes, before much girl talk could occur. Her skirt flew out behind her as she ran toward us, tossing a private smile at one of the dudes behind me.

Today her smile didn't make me nervous, which was odd, because lately everything did. Over the past hour, I'd been breathing more evenly, and my internal monologue hadn't been so dejected. "Your majesty! Master Kerdik and King Urien, may he live forever, have requested you to come back to the palace."

"What's going on?"

She tipped up onto the balls of her feet, her brown shoes dusted with the dirt of the road. "The Untouchables! They've come back for us!"

Montel rose to his feet, calling over his shoulder to the rest of the men. "Did you hear that? Bastien the Bold has returned to help us restore our land!" His fist in the air was met by dozens of enthusiastic cheers.

"Well, that was fast." All of it made me want to run far, far away. "Okay. Thanks for letting me know. I'll be back home tonight once I'm finished with the wall for the day."

Aimee's face fell, and she stopped short of greeting the guy she was excited to see. Jean-Pierre was a nice enough dude, but I'd given him a wide berth, being that his sweat stank like hot garbage. I seemed to make him nervous, which only made him sweat more. "But I was instructed to bring you back straightaway. It seemed the matter was quite urgent."

"I'm sure it'll still be just as urgent tonight." I wasn't looking forward to another grudge match with Kerdik.

She twisted the fabric of her stained apron. "What am I to tell the king? And Master Kerdik, he'll most certainly be displeased."

"You don't have to tell Kerdik anything at all. He'll figure it out on his own easily enough when I don't come home."

"I, um, I don't know, your grace." Whispers broke out among the men, each one speculating on why I didn't want to go greet our hometown heroes. News of my engagement being broken off had spread like wildfire through the land the day after it happened. I'd been getting a mix of looks that ranged from pity to fresh meat. Words like "shamed" and "jilted" followed me like a stigma. I refused to address it, but I felt the sting all the same.

A few beats later, Montel sat next to me on the sideways stump I'd been using as a seat. His voice was low, but firm. "If Master Kerdik requires something of Aimee, she must obey. You don't want her to risk his wrath, do you?"

My shoulders slumped as I took off my gloves and dropped them in the dirt. "Oh, fine. Tell Pascal I didn't want to leave. The job's totally unfinished, but whatever." Our foreman was out with Draper, procuring more supplies, since we were running low on a few things.

"My father knows of your dedication." He stood and

extended his hand to me, hoisting me up and walking as my escort, as Draper had asked him to do. I didn't go anywhere without Montel as my shadow when I was on the job.

"Slower," I requested, wishing for just a little more time before I had to face the man that had broken my heart. I was tanned from too many days in the sun. My fitted tank top and jeans were smeared with dust, mud and smudges of mortar.

Aimee was at my other side, her girl chatter in full swing. "They seemed quite anxious to have you home. Perhaps we should hurry along. Oh, Madigan the Formidable is even bigger than I remember."

"I'll bet."

"Not eager to see your former fiancé?" Montel surmised with a sage smile.

"Right. Yeah, I'd rather be working, not dealing with a bunch of drama."

"Perhaps he's come to ask for your hand again? That would erase so many of the rumors. Then everyone would know that he didn't shame you," Aimee suggested with a teenaged optimism and romanticism about her that I was sorely missing. Girlfriend looked like she was about to start scrawling Rosie... whatever the crap Madigan's last name was, all over her notebook. Rosie the Formidable. That actually had a nice ring to it.

"I'm not sure that's it. I left something with my *Guardien* before they all took off. They're just returning it."

"I'm sure Madigan the Formidable is anxious to get a peek at you. Perhaps you should go up to your chambers, and I'll draw you a bath first? We can sneak you in through the back."

"Is that your fancy way of telling me I look like crap?" I asked her, managing what I hoped looked like a light expression to tease her with. I'd given up on smiling ages ago.

Aimee was horrified. "Oh, no, your grace! You're lovelier than a thousand flowers. Lovelier still than if you had bathed and worn something other than mere peasants' clothing." She cupped her hand over her mouth to stem the flow of foot-in-mouth disease she seemed prone to.

Montel chuckled at my side. "You look like the rest of us laborers, and if he's half the man you deserve, he'll see the beauty in that. A woman working her fingers into blisters to help restore Avalon? A lovelier sight I've never seen."

I shoved my hands in my pockets. "Aw, that's actually really sweet. Thanks, Montel. You're very pretty, too."

He laughed, and the sound was natural on him. "Ha! I guess I can turn in for the day, then. The Avalon Rose said I was pretty. Doesn't get much better than that."

Aimee shot him a narrow-eyed look that told him she thought he was a very bad boy, though he was nearly double her age. "Don't be incorrigible, now. When Madigan the Formidable does ask for her hand again, you'll want to keep that little flirtation under your hat."

I tried not to sigh too obnoxiously. "I'm not marrying Madigan. I'm not marrying anybody. The wall. That's what I'm marrying. That beautiful, sturdy piece of craftsmanship is who's going to carry me over the threshold like the damsel I am."

Montel jutted his chin toward the castle, and the men who waited inside. "I think that wall's going to have some steep competition, your grace."

10

MY BOYFRIEND'S BACK, AND HE'S GOING TO
BE IN TROUBLE

"Lucy, I'm home!" I called throughout the house in a thick Hispanic accent after I waved goodbye to Montel. Aimee scurried away from me, no doubt afraid of the ensuing row Kerdik and I were known to have these days.

Link's operatic voice boomed through the halls from the direction of the parlor, filling my home with the smile and song I'd been missing. "Rosie, I love ye! Rosie, I care. Rosie, without ye, my heart's in despair."

It wasn't just Bastien I'd been living without; it was the trio of misfits who had ditched me outright. Having them back now felt like a fresh slice across the open wound I'd been pretending didn't exist. I kicked off my filthy boots and toed through the halls to the parlor, which was kind of like a super formal living room. The high-backed seats were bedecked with bronze, making the emerald cushions seem to glow with a vibrancy I was too shell-shocked to feel.

There they were with my dad, hanging out like nothing had gone horribly wrong. Well, to be fair, Link was hanging out, lounging on the chaise like a naughty over-sized boy you'd never bring home to meet your parents. He was grinning as he tossed a lively back and forth with my dad about their journey here. Mad was completely upright in his chair, not fiddling or participating in the conversation. As always, he remained on the outskirts of normal life. Kerdik stood behind my dad's chair, bored of the mundane conversations.

When my eyes fell on Bastien, all the denial I'd been constructing into dams to hold my emotions back began to disintegrate – my best efforts reduced to nothing more than a sandcastle that collapsed with laughable ease. He was standing near the double doors, and I was surveying the room from the side entrance, just out of his view. He was unshaven and unwashed, his beard an inch long. His shoulder muscles that had been live wires of capability and brute determination were now slumped with too much tension and defeat. I simultaneously wanted to run to him and run far, far away, so I remained stock still, frozen like a deer with no place to go. "Where is she?" he growled with a touch of desperation.

Mad didn't look in my direction, but jerked his thumb to rat me out. "She's spying from over yonder, like a wee mouse."

I fiddled with the hem of my tank top. It had been white when I'd put in on that morning, but was now a dusty brown and grey. Maybe I should've bathed. Or re-braided my hair. Or eaten lunch. Or worn something nicer.

Link shot up from his chair and barreled over to me, his arms outstretched. "Come here, wee mouse! Kiss your old Link like he's been missing it."

I backed away, wary of falling into the comfort too easily. They'd up and left without much warning, and as soon as Bastien gave me back what was mine, they would go again. I was a woman, which, for all of their talk about taking care of their women, counted for precious little. I was a toy to be cast aside whenever the wind shifted. As much as I understood and accepted it, the whole thing still stung.

Link's eyebrows furrowed. "What's the matter? Didn't ye miss me? I've brought back your prize fighter, plus one fiancé, at your service."

"Thanks. But Mad's not my fiancé anymore, so you don't have to stay."

Link's face soured, and Mad craned his head to watch my lips move, making sure he'd heard me correctly. "'Don't have to stay?' We came all the way from the outskirts of Province 1 to see ye, and tha's all ye can say to me?"

I shrugged. "Um, hi? Nice to see you? I thought you'd left forever? Good you're all still alive?"

Link took a few staggering steps back. "What'd ye do

with my wee Rose? She was warm and knew how to set a man's loins on fire with a crack of her smile."

I stared up at him with a baleful look on my face. "Your loins? Really? That's where we're taking this conversation?"

Urien cleared his throat. "Manners, gentlemen. My daughter's been unwell for too many weeks now. You'll not trouble her with bar humor."

Link's hand flew to my forehead with a frown. "Unwell? Did ye catch something wicked? Ye aren't warm."

Kerdik had been quiet, watching my wary eyes and distrustful expression. "Very well, Bastien. You've seen her. Now you can give her back her *lueur* and be on your way."

"I need to speak with my charge in private," Bastien blurted out to the men, his eyes trained on me like a hawk.

Dad, Draper and Kerdik all watched me for signs of bailing, but I knew I needed to get this over with. I nodded for them to leave, and waited for the room to empty and the doors to shut before I spoke. "Okay. You can give my *lueur* back now."

Bastien gaped at me. "Are you serious? That's all you want to say to me? Do you have any idea what we've been through these past six weeks?"

I wrapped my arms around my middle, wishing I wasn't too filthy to sit down on one of the fancy chairs in the room. "Six weeks? My, how time flies. Feels like you ripped my heart out just yesterday." I was angry, but already I could feel the difference being near him made.

Or, more accurately, being around the part of me he took, and finally brought back. My shoulders relaxed and my chest moved without the pressure I'd been breathing through for too long.

Bastien didn't bother with small talk or beating around the bush. "I shouldn't have gone in for that first drink. I don't stop at one when I'm in a downward spiral like that. I don't even remember cheating on you, but if you say it happened, I believe you." He waited for my response, but I kept the acid tucked inside of me. "I got drunk, and the bartender offered to let me sleep it off in one of the beds upstairs, so that's all I meant to do. I'm sorry. Believe me, of all the things I am, sorry is the biggest one."

My gaze cut to him, and for a second my glare didn't seem worth the cost it took from me to take in the scope of his face. He was too beautiful, so handsome my heart ached. He had bags under his eyes, too, and looked about as desperate and lost as I felt. His face was thinner, his movements not as certain. "The bartender told me himself that you had one of the girls up there. I saw her climb off of you with my own two eyes. Ruby's been spreading it around town how big your dick is, and how the two of you went at it all night. She's the envy of all the single women in Province 9. Got herself a night with Bastien the Bold. Apparently, you were her best lay ever. Coming from a prostitute, that's quite the compliment. Congrats."

Bastien's voice was contrite, and he sounded like a lost

boy who'd woken up in a life he didn't recognize. "I don't remember a second of it. Are you sure it happened?"

"When Draper and I fished you out of that place, you came down stinking like overripe vagina and beer."

His nose crinkled in distaste at my harsh phrasing. *Whatever.* I was in no mood to tiptoe around the reality of it all. Bastien held up his hands. "I haven't looked at another woman since I kissed you the first time, and probably long before that. Honest, Daisy."

My fists clenched at my sides. "No! Don't call me 'Daisy', like you're on my side. Don't talk about when we kissed. That's so far forgotten by now."

"I've been trying to get back to you ever since you sent me away. You shipped me off unconscious, by the way, with no say in any of it."

The sound of his voice was both honey and astringent vinegar to my ears, warming and freezing my heart simultaneously. I tried to keep my voice even. "I would've given you all the say in the world, but you were too drunk to speak up. I don't need a *Guardien* who barfs up a belly full of beer while I'm getting choked out mere inches away from him."

I could tell my words cut him, a tortured look of self-flagellation surfacing in his caramel eyes. "That's on me, yes."

"You ducked out long before I sent you away. You should've tried to come back that very first time you stayed out all night, drinking yourself sick while I waited at home for you like a chump." I glared at him, remembering enough pieces of who I was, so I could assemble enough pride to speak my piece. "I'm not the girl who sits at home, waiting for her boyfriend to call. You tried to make me that girl, and I don't forgive you for it. I thought you were out rebuilding Avalon to make our home a safer place, but you were spending your nights in a whorehouse! I could barely walk after being stabbed three times, and you were buried deep in some other woman!"

Bastien held up his hands. "You're totally right on that part. That was completely my fault. I went off the deep end when Roland admitted all he did to you. I've seen Mad work before, but knowing that was all happening to the friend I've known since childhood? It was too much, Rosie."

I pursed my lips before speaking. "No one's trying to take your grief away from you. Go grieve, by all means. Just don't pretend to be on the job while you are. You left me wide open for an attack every day you chose to drown your sorrows alone." I shook my head at him. "I would've understood all of it. I would've listened to you and held you through the worst parts, but you confided in the bartender, and some other woman's vagina!"

"I didn't mean to cheat on you!" he shouted.

"Whatever we had? It wasn't a relationship, if that's how you deal when you're in pain. You're definitely not a man who should be guarding anyone. Stop me if I'm wrong, really."

Bastien lowered his head and turned his chin from side to side, his shoulders slumped. "You're not wrong. I'm not asking you to brush that off. I behaved..." I could tell he was fishing for the right word. "My captain would have called my behavior disgraceful, and he wouldn't be wrong. I disgraced you, your throne, and us."

My mouth fell open at his debasement. It was like, the fiftieth time that he'd been humble and repentant instead of defensive. Bastien was sorry, though by now, I wasn't sure how much that mattered to us. For him, however, it was a solid win, personal growth-wise.

Bastien wasn't finished voicing all the things I'd been yelling at him in my head. "I'm your *Guardien*, and I let my personal stuff cloud that out. More important than that, I'm your boyfriend, and I didn't talk to you about what was going on with me. I just checked out." He rubbed his forehead. "I'm not used to having a woman around. I'm not good at relationships."

My voice was quiet, but firm. "Well, you don't have to worry about that. You're not in a relationship anymore. After you give me back my *lueur*, you can go on with your happy hermit ways."

Bastien kept his eyes on the floor, acting like an animal who was submitting to the king of the jungle – or queen, as it were. It was strange and a little off-putting to see a strong man so humbled. "I had a bad week. One week where you couldn't count on me. One week off the job when my close friend died a horrible death after stabbing me in the back. You can't cut me a little slack over one lousy week?"

I shoved my hands in my pockets, hiding the mark on my wrist that threatened my temper. "I almost died in that one week. And I would've totally been cool with you taking a week for yourself, had you asked me. You didn't talk to me at all. You just checked out." I shook my head. "I don't want to do this. I'm filthy, so I'm going to go wash up and change. You can leave the *lueur* with Kerdik or my dad."

I turned to leave, but Bastien was at my side in the next breath, his hand on the door to keep it shut. "No." I'd forgotten the feel of his breath on my skin, but my nerves lit with new life under his simple bull-like exhale. He was so much taller than me, bulkier. His arms had been my safe place, once upon a better time.

I tried to straighten and reclaim my hold on my independence. "Excuse me? No, you won't give me back what's mine? You'd actually keep me not being able to sleep, anxious as all get-out, and broken how I am? You're a real piece of work, dude."

Bastien raised his voice a little when his frustration peaked. "Don't call me 'dude', like I'm some guy you don't belong with."

My teeth ground together. "Give me back my *lueur*. I'm exhausted, and I want to feel like myself again. I thought it was being away from you that made me feel lost, but it was being away from the part of myself you took with you. Give it back."

"You'll feel like yourself if I'm near. You've only been anxious because I couldn't get to you soon enough. I felt the same thing. Haven't been able to keep much food down without you around."

"My sympathies. It's been six weeks that I've been in the same boat, while helping rule a province and rebuild a friggin' wall. Give it back to me, and then go on your merry way. Eat a whole elephant, for all I care."

"Rosie, please! For one second, pretend like I'm the guy you fell in love with. Pretend you understand that when a man's messed up, he doesn't always think straight."

"What a luxury it is to be a man." I met his eyes, not bothering to hide the hurt that slashed across my heart at the sight of him so close, yet still eons away. "When Mad nearly murdered me, you could've saved my life with a single word. You were too far gone, and it could've cost me my life. Go on as many benders as you want. I won't gamble on you anymore. Not when the dude who wants me dead is still out there."

Bastien's chest puffed, his face mutating from wounded puppy to guard dog in a breath. "What are you talking about?"

"Nothing that concerns you at all."

"The man who controlled Mad was after controlling Mad, not hurting you. You were just the nearest person."

He was vocalizing the logic he'd no doubt worked out weeks ago. It was the same logic I'd had before the hooded man held me at knifepoint not too long ago. "No. No, Rosie. He wanted to use Mad as a weapon. It's someone from his past he thought was dead. It's got nothing to do with you."

I crossed my arms over my chest. "Tell that to the knife he sliced me with just a couple weeks ago."

11

THE BOYS ARE BACK IN TOWN

Bastien reached out and gripped my shoulders, squeezing too tight out of genuine fear that was mingled with rage. "Someone stabbed you?!" Then he reached for the door and flung it open, bellowing out into the hallway, "Rosie's been stabbed! Get Remy! Jean-Luc! Help!"

I rolled my eyes when the five men came charging in from the kitchen. I held up my hands. "Bastien's overreacting. I was cut like, a couple weeks ago, not like, while you were standing in the room with me. Jeez."

Link had a mouthful of chicken that rolled around for everyone to see when he put words to his shock. "Where were ye stabbed? Show me now!"

Kerdik's shoulders fell. "Oh, that's what the commotion's about? Jean-Luc had a look at her. She's all sewn up."

Mad stepped toward me with menace in his glinting

eyes. "Who attacked my bride?" It wasn't love, but territory that drove his thick eyebrows to push together and his voice to deepen.

I guffawed at him. "Um, nobody. You don't have a bride. I'm not your fiancée. You asked for your ring back, and everybody friggin' knows it."

Link snatched up my hand to display my wrist, but I slapped him away. "Ye wear our mark. No one takes a blade to one of our ladies and lives to brag about it."

I glared at the three of them, feeling ganged up on, and like somehow the upper hand had been stolen from me. "First off, I'm no one's lady anymore, so I'm free to be stabbed by whoever feels like it. Second, what good is your stupid mark if none of you are around to enforce it? You all left me, and you can go right back where you came from – out of my sight."

It was as if I hadn't spoken. Mad glowered at me, like I was the one who'd done the stabbing. "Show me where he stuck ye. Was it the same voice who controlled me?"

"Same dude, I'm guessing. I didn't see his face either time. He was wearing that same black cloak. Éireland accent. Sliced me across the back of my hip. It's healed up fine, and I don't need a bunch of older brothers who're going to flake when I need them to stick around. I already have a brother, and he got me out of there well enough without some useless tattoo that means friggin' nothing."

Link and Bastien balked at me, but Mad held my gaze. He didn't like to be touched, but there were times his eye contact felt almost like a physical jolt. He was tall – easily six and a half feet, but when his temper was stimulated, he seemed impossibly more gigantic, swelling to the size of the Stay Puft Marshmallow Man, while I shrank to the stature of one of the frightened Munchkins from the *Wizard of Oz.* "My mark means tha no one touches ye! My mark means ye never have to look over your shoulder again for the rest of your life. Ye could stand right in front of Morgan le Fae, and she wouldn't be able to touch ye with my mark!"

I tried to remind myself that I wasn't a Munchkin, but a woman who knew how to stand on her own well enough. Having the little bit of myself back that I'd given to Bastien made me stand straighter, finding myself when I'd been lost for so long. "Tell it to my sweet little scar." I pointed in Mad's face, shooting straight with him so there was no room for arguments. "You bailed on me, and everyone in the kingdom was talking about it. They know you left, and that you're not coming back for me. I know our engage-ment was for show, but breaking it off was real to everyone who you were supposed to scare away. Not to mention all the rumors and talk about me being publicly shamed by you." I scowled at Bastien. "You know how you put me on hold for Reyn's sister, so Rachelle wouldn't be shamed? Consider this my apology for if I ever gave you a hard time about it. I'm glad she had her honor intact until the end. Me? Not so much." Many of the women still couldn't hold my gaze.

Mad sneered at me, as if that was an adequate response. He ripped his gold ring off his finger and shoved it at me. "There. Now it's fixed."

I guffawed, not bothering to hold back my tendency toward the obnoxious when I was insulted. "Don't bother. You're not staying." I dropped the ring into Mad's hand and looked to Link and Bastien. "None of you are. Bastien, give me back my *lueur*, and you can go back to your cabin in the woods with your boys."

Bastien's eyes glinted at me, his humility vanishing as anger pushed it out of the way. "You know what? No. I took this job, and yeah, I had a sucky week where I dropped the ball after my friend of twenty years died. But I swore I'd protect you and your household, and that still stands. You're not getting rid of me just to prove a point."

I spluttered my anger, unable to come up with a coherent response. I turned to my dad, who was standing in the hallway with Kerdik and Draper. He surveyed the scene as a wise king would – gathering the facts before he intervened. "I've no problem with a *Guardien* living up to his duty." Then he turned to Bastien. "I've a problem with a *Guardien* who drinks while he's supposed to be protecting my daughter. I trust you've tasted your last sip of alcohol?"

Bastien held the king's stare, his chest broadening as his chin lifted like the regal lumberjack he was. "On my honor, your majesty. If I drink again, I'll give Rosie back her *lueur* without a fight."

Urien nodded once, as if the whole thing was decided. "Very well. Am I to understand that with one of you comes the other two?"

Link and Mad nodded, but Bastien answered for them. "Untouchables go where they like. Only I'm bound to Rosie, not them. If they help, it's because they want to, and it'll be appreciated as such."

Bastien was polishing up his speech because my dad was around. Otherwise, there's no way he'd be throwing around proper phrases like "as such." I wanted to shove him hard and storm out of the room for somehow getting my dad to go along with him on this. I stayed in place, though, acting like the princess I'd been marketed as.

Urien reached out and shook Bastien's hand. "Very good. I'll have Aimee show you to your rooms, so you can get settled in. Feel free to make yourselves at home, but we're not bringing outside people into the castle anymore. My daughter's been attacked. I'll be holding court on the front steps at night to make sure my daughter can sleep without worry she'll be gutted whenever she lets her guard down."

I shut my eyes. "Great. Now that visual's in my head."

Link gave me a snotty sibling look that Judah had on occasion doled out when he was being a brat. "Grand. I think I'll set up in Rosie's room. For the wee kitten's protection, of course." He pecked my cheek when I gasped indignantly, and then walked on out of the room so he could pretend my wrath was imaginary.

"Ho no, you don't!" I called after him down the hall, furious at his haughty laughter that echoed off the stone walls. "Get your stuff out of my space! I'm serious, Link. I'll throw your pack out the window if it lands even in the air surrounding my bedroom."

Mad reached out unexpectedly and snatched at my face, clutching my jaw. His firm grip was on the borderline of bruising. His imposed authority made me want to kick him, but after a few seconds of his penetrating stare, I stilled. "I shouldn't have left ye. I'll make good on it all." Then he exited with no further explanation.

Kerdik had watched the entire scene unfold without intervening, but when Bastien made to leave with his pack and go upstairs to settle in, he pressed his hand to Bastien's chest. "I healed you and gave you abilities you haven't even begun to understand yet."

Bastien nodded respectfully. "Thank you."

"I didn't do it for you; I did it so that Rosie would be safe. Do not disappoint me again with your foolishness. Urien is far more rational and forgiving than I am."

Bastien's gaze hardened, but he didn't argue. "Yes, sir." Then Bastien snuck me a wounded look before he left me with my father, my brother, my green friend, and my fury.

12

AN UNKINDNESS OF RAVENS

With the return of the Untouchables came order like the palace had never known. Though the guys hadn't seemed overly concerned before, the reappearance of our hooded villain brought out the military man in all three of them. Commands were given, men were solicited, and pretty soon, we had a makeshift army that Mad had taken it upon himself to break in. Though it seemed Avalon was predisposed to fighting, Mad gave their fists and swords purpose and accuracy. The whole thing was actually kind of impressive, but I wasn't about to break the stalemate and tell him. We were content to ignore each other, so I kept my distance from him as much as I could. I had my *lueur* back in the vicinity, so my moods weren't so acerbic, and I started to feel marginally more myself. Myself these days, though, was quieter after all I'd been through.

Building the wall went much slower, now that Mad was training the willing men all night long. He did drills with them, marched them through the region and set them to work rebuilding houses that were in disrepair. By the time the sun rose and they were given time to rest their sore muscles, they weren't as enthusiastic about lugging bricks around to the wall.

"You're mixing mortar today. I heard Pascal tell you that." Bastien frowned down at me as I hefted the wheelbarrow filled with bricks, and started ambling toward the wall.

I knew Bastien was telling Pascal not to let me work too much, but I decided not to call him on it. "The mortar's as mixed as it should be. The brick hauling is falling behind, so I'm helping where I'm needed, if that's alright." There was a sparrow perched on my shoulder who chirped in my ear little songs about twigs. My new pet bird was supposed to be filling me in on the goings on of the village, but Emil often got distracted. He was a good singer, though, so I didn't mind. I'd taught him the tune of one of my favorite Lost and Forgotten songs, "You Never Knew Me", which Emil totally rocked. He was better than a radio, for sure.

Bastien grumbled about me being difficult, but he didn't dare say anything more about it. We had hit an unspoken agreement of limiting the hostility between us. It was a fragile truce, but we tried to respect it all the same. "Just be careful. Jean-Luc told you to slow down. Don't think he doesn't write stuff down for me."

I parked the wheelbarrow near where the guys were working, and gave Montel a fist bump in lieu of an actual greeting. When I addressed Bastien, I tried to stand my ground without being snippy. I kept my chin pointed downward as I spoke with as much grace as I could muster. "I know my limits, Bastien. I'm working at the same speed as the rest of the guys."

"They don't need to sleep like you do."

Instead of responding to Bastien, I spun on my heel and sauntered away to go stir mortar like a good little girl. It was actually a fine job, but once it was mixed, it only needed the occasional stir. I didn't like how it felt to sit idly while everyone else was working up a good sweat.

Bastien visited me when I sat back down to stir the heavy open kettle. "I'm not trying to piss you off. I just wanted to make sure you don't hurt yourself."

I gave him a curt bob of my head, but said nothing.

"You think Mad's done scouting the perimeter?"

I shrugged, and then took a sip of water from my canteen. "I haven't seen him in days. He's pissed at me. Either that, or he's just super into the job."

Bastien added more water to the mix, since it was starting to clump. "He's pissed at himself. He didn't realize he'd be hurting you by leaving. Especially with the whole public shaming thing with your engagement. Mad doesn't... He has a hard time understanding people. More than most. Usually his Untouchable status makes that worry go away. He's not used to caring who he hurts, but he loves you. He's upset he got it all wrong, so he's afraid to be around you. Doesn't want to hurt you again."

I blinked at Bastien. "Are you serious? He doesn't have to... I didn't mean for him to internalize it like that."

"You meant for him to understand that leaving was the wrong move, and that there were consequences to his decision. People assume he feels nothing, but when something finally does get through, it cuts him deeper than most." Bastien cast me a humble glance. "So when you do see him again, you might want to give him something that lets him know he didn't break you."

"He didn't break me."

"I know he didn't. *I* did." Bastien didn't leave room for arguments, and I had none to offer. His shoulders curved, doing that self-protecting thing he often did when he assumed life might attack. "Everything I did... You were right to send me away." He lowered his head in shame. "I got our baby murdered. I was passed out right next to where Abraham Lincoln was probably crying for me to save him." He ran his hand over his forehead, and kept his eyes downward. I could tell this wasn't the first time he'd felt this stab of guilt.

I didn't say anything to try and assuage the self-contemplation, but let him feel it. The others gave me a wide berth when Bastien was around, so our conversation remained private. I didn't know what to do, so I settled for resting my hand on his spine to let him know that even though I wasn't his girlfriend anymore, I was still a safe place for him. "We buried him in the woods with Hamish. I can take you there, if you like."

Bastien's head bobbed, and he kept his eyes on his knees. "My old man was like that. One drink, then he'd slam ten more. Spent a fair amount of my childhood cleaning puke off the floor." His lashes swept shut in self-loathing. "I didn't want that life for you – the man you count on, passed out from drinking when you need him most."

I kept my mouth shut, unsure how to handle Bastien's closely guarded childhood gracefully without making him crawl back into his turtle shell. I rubbed his back to soothe the ache that had been festering inside of him for far too long.

Bastien slumped against me, and then reached across my lap to gather up my other hand in his, holding my knuckles to his cheek. "Link and Mad managed to knock some sense into me. I'm not an addict. I mean, I can go months without touching a drop. Years, maybe. But once I start, I can't stop." He shook his head at himself. "I'm not going to drink again, even if you never take me back. Abraham Lincoln counted on me, and I let him down. That was my wakeup call. If you see a drink in my hand, don't try to talk me out of it. I want you to walk right up to me and punch me in the face. Mad and Link were given the same instructions." He pushed my knuckles to his cheek to demonstrate.

"I think I can manage that. For what it's worth, I'm

proud of you for admitting you have a problem, and doing something about it. We have whole support groups up in Common for stuff like that. I wish Avalon had them for you."

He brought my hand to his lips and kissed the dirt-spattered tips of my fingers one by one. "Don't be proud. I'm too ashamed for anyone to be proud of me." He cleared his throat and stood. "I need to go check for threats. I won't be out of your sight, though, so don't worry about any attacks. I've got this." He met my eyes, and I could see the humility replacing the brazen attitude he'd displayed when we'd first met. "I've got you."

True to his word, he didn't let me out of his sight. As frustrating as that was in the beginning, we were finding a rhythm as time gave us the grace to put certain things into a more merciful light.

By the time the day was called because we'd lost the sunlight, I was nice and exhausted. Having my *lueur* in the vicinity gave me my appetite back, and had helped me sleep deeper. I wasn't looking over my shoulder quite so much, either.

That evening, I waited in the line for my meal in the Town Square with the rest of the laborers in Avalon, but Link did his usual cutting to the front and brought Bastien and me bowls of stew, so we didn't have to wait. I wanted to protest again that it was rude, but if he hadn't cared the first six times I'd warned him, I knew he wasn't about to change any time soon. "Thanks, Link."

"Ye look like ye might fall over. Have a seat with your old Link. Tell me about the wall. Come on and sit with us, Bastien."

Of the trio, Link had been the first to break through my icy tundra. It was too much effort to stay angry at him when he was determined we would get along. He'd employed jokes, frustration, flattery, and finally sincere apologies. It was the apologies without the added excuses that did it. Now he was making it his mission in life to get Bastien and me to reconcile. There was something sweet about the eternal optimist in Link. He'd seen so many brutalities in his life, but he would barrel through them all and rearrange them until his world was in an order he approved of. You had to admire that.

Link sat on the second step of the platform, his long legs stretching out next to mine as I sat on the bottom step. "So, tell me about the wall. Is it still a wall? Tell old Link all about the grand things tha make it a wall."

"Well, bricks, for one. Then we mix the mortar with unicorn tears and rainbow dust. Then I wave my princess arms over the cauldron and whisper the magic words: 'I like it when you call me Big Poppa. So wave your hands in the air, like you's a true player. Because I see some ladies tonight that should be having my baby – baby.'"

Link loved Common rap the more blatantly filthy the lyrics got. He threw his head back in a laugh. "Ho! That's even grander than the one about your arse."

Bastien's head whipped to the two of us before he

settled in next to me on my other side, giving us a healthy foot of space. "Maybe that's not the best thing to be singing about."

Emil chirped in my ear that he thought I had a lovely voice. I stroked his feathers with my pinky before spooning some of the hot stew. It was thick and comforting, as it always was. I had been sharing my chunks of beef with Draper, but my brother was busy chatting up one of the bustier women who giggled at his jokes, like they were the first jokes that ever were. Instead, I spooned a hunk of meat into Link's bowl, who chomped at it greedily.

Link leaned down when I made to give him another piece. "I think our Bastien could use the meat more than me today. He looks a wee bit piqued."

Link was always trying to get the two of us to reconcile. Truthfully, I wasn't even all that mad anymore, but I didn't trust Bastien the way I used to, and that made things cool instead of congenial.

Instead of ignoring Link's prodding, I decided to at least be friendly. "Bastien, did you want my beef?"

The olive branch was small, but it was the first one I'd offered him since they'd returned more than a week ago. Bastien nodded and held out his bowl to me, inching closer so that when I leaned over to make sure I didn't spill anything, he was able to brush his cheek to mine.

I'd been so careful not to touch him at all. I didn't want the feelings to still be there, burning beneath my icy exterior. The simple scratch from his scruff on my soft and dirty skin made me freeze, indulging in the contact as if it were a guilty dessert. I didn't have any business being so near him, and yet, here I was.

People could see us, our cheeks pressed together in hushed desire to finally be near the one we'd been sure we'd lost forever. His whisper tickled my ear with a gentle, "I love you, and I'm so sorry. Please, Rosie."

My breathing hitched from the touch, coupled with the words he'd said to me no less than four times every day since they'd returned. There was something different about the simple plea today, and it drew me in, rather than reaffirming that the barrier around my heart needed barbed wire and angry guards to keep Bastien from invading again.

His piney scent that was dipped in a hint of cinnamon drew me in, and after everything, I still wasn't sure if that was a good thing or a bad one. He was dirty from working beside me all day. He'd given me just enough space that I didn't have to talk to him, but not so much that anyone could attack me again. It was strange, Bastien's band of protection. I was never sure if I was safer with it or without.

I didn't have the words to speak my heart, mostly because I didn't quite understand the many conflicting emotions myself. Instead I dipped my head and spooned around for another chunk of meat in the thick broth, lifting it from my bowl and offering him the bite.

Bastien slid so close that our thighs were touching. I

was keenly aware of every move, every breath, every spot on my body that was in contact with his. He opened his mouth and let me feed him, and for all the confusion between us, our silence held a perfect synchronicity that was too hard for us to deny it existed.

I was still angry that he'd cheated. I wasn't sure what to do with that frustration, though. I wasn't sure what to do, period. My *lueur* stayed tucked inside of him, drawing me closer, like a magnet I had no business resisting.

Emil hopped off of my shoulder and landed on Bastien's, nuzzling his scruff with the top of his head, using it to preen his feathers. "No fair," I complained. "He was my bird first."

Bastien bumped his shoulder to mine so that Emil had twice the space to play around. "What's this little guy's name?"

"Emil. The flock sent him to watch me for the day."

Bastien reached up to stroke the bird's feathers, and then took a chance by brushing his knuckles to my cheek.

I felt the heat rise in my skin, burning where he touched me, so I had to act fast and spackle shtick in where too much vulnerability was exposed. "I know what you're thinking."

"I highly doubt that. You would've punched me if you knew what it did to me to touch your skin."

I swallowed and relished the feel of his rough knuckle on my cheek. "You're thinking Emil's got stronger muscles than you, but your brains are the same size. You're right on both counts."

He didn't fall for my diversion, but met my eyes with seriousness that couldn't be batted away, even with the dumbest of jokes. There was an intensity that burned there, soaking me in with gentleness from a man who knew real loss. "I say we try harder to get it right this time."

I was about to open my mouth and reply – with what, I don't know.

"Let's get out of here," Bastien suggested.

"You're still eating your stew."

Bastien tipped the bowl to his lips and drained it in a few seconds. He wiped his mouth on his flannel sleeve and stood, taking my empty bowl and hoisting me up. I kept my voice low. "Um, I'm pretty sure people will notice if we leave together."

Bastien took a chance and coiled his arm around my back, drawing me closer than a friendly distance. "I hope so. Like I said, we'll get it right this time. We won't be together behind closed doors while you're fake engaged to my friend. This is what I should've done from the beginning." He shook his head, ignoring the whispers that were spreading around us at our relationship-like body language. "You were right to throw me out, Ro. But I'm back now." He leaned in and played the game like a cheater, whispering in my ear just to make me melt. "Take me back."

It was a thing of luck we were interrupted, though I

didn't expect the culprit to be an unkindness of ravens soaring down and chirping in my face. The villagers had grown somewhat used to the animals talking to me, but a whole flock was a visual that made them all inch away or stumble back. "Hey, guys. What'd I miss?"

They were all talking at once, which, when you factor in that they spoke in a high-pitched birdy squawk, it made the whole thing totally confusing. All I got was "water" and "the mother". Several started pecking at my canteen, flapping their wings as they tried to communicate... something.

Draper abandoned the woman he'd been chatting up and made a beeline to me, standing on the other side of the birds with his arms crossed over his shoulders. "What is it, Ro?"

I set down my bowl and held up my hands, motioning for the nearest one to perch on my wrist. "Okay, just one of you tell me what's got you all in a tizzy."

"The water! The water's killing off our young! Something's wrong with the water! Don't drink it!"

I tugged my canteen off my belt and opened it, peering inside for a floating skull and crossbones or something. I sniffed it curiously. "I've been drinking it all day, and I don't feel any different."

"Poison! It's been poisoned!"

It was then that something landed like a rock on the ground a few feet from me. I jumped, but the birds only hopped animatedly around the intrusion they'd apparently been expecting. I got down on all fours and crawled forward to examine the black mass that had fallen from the ravens circling overhead. My hand covered my mouth, stifling my unfiltered gasp.

"Don't touch it, Rosie!" Draper craned his neck to gape up at the ravens circling above us.

I focused on the spokesbird who was now perched on my forearm. "When did this happen?"

"It's been happening for four nights now, but we only just figured out the cause. Help us! We can't live without water."

I was careful not to touch the dead bird with my bare hands. "Link, do you have a handkerchief?"

"Aye, but it's a wee bit manky."

"That's fine. We have to take this bird back to the castle and show Dad. He needs to see that the baby birds are dying."

Would that I had kept the conversation with the bird to myself. The palpable fear started to rise all around me, rippling out from the spot where I stood in waves of gasps. "Nobody drink the water! The birds are dying from it!" Montel called out, spreading the word like wildfire. It was good that they would all stop drinking the water, but not so great that panic and shrieks started to fill the air.

13

MADNESS IN TOWN SQUARE

 wrapped the bird in Link's green bandana and scrambled up the steps, trying to gain everyone's attention, and failing miserably. Bastien shouted for them all to listen, but anxiety was running high now. With no better option, I turned and gave the overlarge gong a sidekick to rival Chuck Norris (actually, it was pretty sloppy, but in my mind, I was Avalon's version of Chuck Norris for that brief second). That seemed to get enough of them to turn around so that I could take the floor. "Everyone, listen up. The birds are saying something's wrong with the water, and it's killing off their young. It's been going on for four days, so we've all had some of the water by now." I kicked the gong again like a ninja when audible sobs rose louder than I could talk. "Don't panic. Birds have smaller bodies than us, so whatever's hurting them will take a lot longer to hurt us. But for now, don't drink the water. I'll go run this little guy back to King Urien, and we'll see what we can do." I looked around at the tens of thousands of people, but knew that there were hundreds of thousands in our province. "I need the dudes who've been working on the wall to come up here for a special job. Quick, now! Everyone else, head home. Don't freak out, but don't drink the water, either. Just lay low tonight. When we figure this out, Dad, Draper or I will come back here to the Town Square to let you all know what's what."

I motioned to Link, Montel and Bastien, and out of nowhere, Mad was standing behind me. "Montel, could you take Draper back to the castle? I'll be there in a second." I locked eyes with my buddy, communicating silently that I needed Draper away from the commotion to be sure he was safe. From what? I wasn't totally sure.

"I'm not leaving without you, obviously," Draper spouted off with a sour expression.

I pursed my lips, but didn't argue. "Fine." I pulled the five guys in for a huddle as the men I'd been working with gathered to the foot of the platform. Link clapped me on the shoulder. "Tha's the way to handle a crowd before they get out of sorts. Send them to their homes so they can't spread more talk and panic."

"Thanks, Link. I need you three to organize the guys and send them out into the land to warn everyone about the water. We can't have people dying off just because they didn't know. Can you divide them up and assign them specific areas, so that every house is covered?"

"Aye, wee Rose. We can do tha, no problem."

Bastien shook his head. "Give me the bird. I'm going with you, and you're not holding something that's been poisoned. I'll take it."

I waved off his concern. "I can make it back home with Montel and Draper. It's not like I'm going to drop dead along the way."

Bastien pointed two fingers from his eyes to mine, focusing us both. "Not out of my sight. There's still someone out looking for you, and chaos like this is the best time to strike. Mad? Link? You got this?"

"Aye." Link answered, and Mad nodded. Link spun around and clapped his hands together, calling to the workers who'd gathered, and splitting them up according to territories.

Bastien and Draper each put an arm around me, sandwiching me in, with Montel on Draper's other side. Bastien's hand coveted the small of my back, and the familiar feel of his territorial touch sent a flood of girlish gooiness through me that I tried to quickly suppress. The two men moved forward, shoulders hunched inward to deflect any attacks that might come my way. I felt like I was some A-list celebrity with her bodyguards. Only instead of a designer purse, I was holding a dead bird. Totally surreal. The three tried to escort me through the crowd that had somehow gone from eating and hanging out together to a stampede that left everyone scared. They all wanted to get home to their loved ones and make sure no one was dead.

We made it a few feet from the platform when I saw a kid no more than seven years old get totally trampled by several people who were in a hurry, and plowed the poor girl over. I shrieked, pressed the dead bird into Bastien's chest and broke from the guys, running to the little girl. "You mow her down and don't even stop? Obnoxious!" I scolded the people who kept running past. From the time I spotted her to the time I scooped her up off the dirt, five people had stepped on her. Poor baby had tears in her eyes and a bloody nose. I held her trembling body to mine, cradling her as if she was a toddler as I stood. Her legs wrapped easily around my waist, holding onto me for dear life.

The three guys were a few steps behind, but caught up with fresh reprimands coming at me from all sides. I didn't pay them any mind, but glanced around for the girl's parents. "What's your name, sweetie?" I asked in as gentle a voice as I could muster.

Her black hair was pin straight and fell back from her face. She was thin, but not too bony, and had a large scar from her temple to her chin. I didn't recognize her from the soccer games I'd organized in the dungeon, but there were new people coming into the province all the time. "A-A-Annabelle, your majesty." Her tears seemed frozen on her face as she gaped at me, just now realizing whose arms she was in. "The Avalon Rose!"

"Yup. Where are you hurt, Annabelle? I see this scrape on your elbow. Man, you're brave. I would've been howling like a baby if I'd taken a dive like that. You sure you don't play football on the side?" I scanned the crowd for her parents, but no one was frantically crying, "Where's my daughter?"

Draper motioned toward the platform, and Mad barreled through the crowd without apology or hesitation. It was the beauty of having a linebacker on your team.

Mad and I hadn't spoken more than a few sentences since he'd returned, but I didn't waste time as I handed the girl to him. "What are ye doing? Don't give me tha!" He tried to shove her back into my arms.

"This is Annabelle. She got trampled, but I don't see her parents. Can you keep an eye on her until her parents come? If you can't find them, bring Annabelle to the palace after the dust settles."

Mad held Annabelle out from his body under her back and knees like a human sacrifice, clearly having never held a child before. "It's plain she doesn't like me! Take her back home with ye."

"Her parents will be looking for her. I can't just steal someone's kid."

"But... But... I... Ye can't leave me with this thing!" I could see by the sweat beading on Mad's forehead that he wasn't trying to be a jerk; he was just totally scared of kids.

Bastien chucked his friend's shoulder. "You can do this. Just take her to the platform so her parents can see her."

Annabelle was higher off the ground in Mad's arms, and I could tell the additional height startled her. "Grand," he said with a heavy layer of fear and sarcasm. "Now run to the palace and don't stop for anymore wee ones."

I bent his elbow and gently pushed her closer to him until the side of her body was resting against his broad chest. "Hold her like that, otherwise you might drop her."

Mad grimaced at the child in his arms as she clung to his shirt, which I could tell he hadn't been expecting. She looked slightly more afraid of falling than she did of Mad. "Uh... Um... I shouldn't be holding a kid!" Then he whirled around, ripping a screech from Annabelle. "Who belongs to this girl? Come on, now. Fess up."

I rolled my eyes at the caveman as Bastien and Draper whirled me around and marched me toward the castle, with Montel watching our backs.

Even as we put distance between the Town Square, I could hear Madigan growl, "Alright, now! Don't leave me with a girl, people. Anybody!"

14

PRIDE AND POTIONS

The birds followed me all the way to the castle, watching their lost baby and making sure they didn't need to peck anyone's eyes out if they messed with me. Birds loved easily, and I adored them for it. "Your minions can't come inside, Rosie," Bastien said as he slammed the front doors shut.

Montel breathed a sigh of relief that he'd gotten us inside, but now that he was here, he looked embarrassed. "Apologies, princess. I didn't think. I just followed you inside. I'll take my leave."

"Nonsense. Do you need to get home?"

Montel shrugged. "Not really. My father heard the announcement, and it's just him and me in our household. He saw me leave with Draper."

"Then you're welcome to stay." I craned my neck to yell down the hall. "Dad!" When he didn't answer, I trotted toward the throne room. Though we didn't hold court inside anymore, it was where he went to do his best thinking. I loved the idea of him pacing the throne room with all his brilliant ideas and plans for Avalon formulating in his sharp mind. "Dad!" I called as I rounded the corner.

"Yes, darling." Urien came out of the throne room, predictably doing his pacing and pondering. I loved that I was getting to know his little habits. "What's troubling you?"

"Just missing your face," I said, gazing up at him with admiration. "Oh, and here's a dead bird. They think the water's been poisoned." I opened up the green bandana and showed him the evidence.

"Oh, my. Let me see the little fellow." He was careful not to touch the bird, but examined the feathers, the nails, the beak and the glazed-over eyes carefully. His lashes shut in frustration. "Why must Kerdik always choose the most inconvenient times to go on holiday?"

My nose scrunched, like there was a gross stench in the air. "Huh? Where's Kerdik? He can't be gone. He wouldn't leave without telling me."

"Kerdik does a great many things without approval or consult from anyone. He's gone, though he'll most likely return when he tires of his respite."

My mouth fell open. "No. I mean, that's not possible. We were supposed to go bowling in the dungeon tonight. He wouldn't bail on me. We had plans."

Urien gave me this sad look of pity, as if I'd told him I

could build a flying machine out of old candy bar wrappers, and take us to the moon on vacation. "Perhaps I'm wrong. Perhaps he'll be back in a few minutes, but in the off chance I'm correct in my assumption that we're on our own, we need to get to the bottom of this." He folded the bird back up in the bandana and pinched the bridge of his nose. "If the birds are certain that it's the water supply, then it's already too late. I think I know what this is."

Draper's hand found my shoulder. "What? If it's in the water, then it could be anything. It might take us weeks to figure this all out. And without fresh water, we just don't have that long."

Urien peeled back the edge of the green bandana to show us the poor baby's frozen feet. "Do you see the black edges on the nails? And look at this." Using the cloth, he pried back a few feathers, exposing the flesh beneath. I expected to see pale skin at the root of the coal feathers, but instead there were gray and black spots that protruded out from the skin, almost like miniature boils.

"What happened to her?" Montel asked. He'd grown a soft spot for my animals, as they often accompanied us on the wall.

"It's the *mort noire* root. It's been introduced to our water supply, which means someone ground up *mort noire* and dropped it in our wells."

Draper postured. "But that would mean there's a spy among us. Morgan couldn't have done this herself."

Urien nodded gravely. "Indeed. This much we already

knew, though. We just assumed the cloaked man's only mission was to take out Rosie. Now we know he means our entire region harm. If it is him, in fact." He sighed and closed his eyes. "Or perhaps we have two foes with two separate agendas."

"How do we undo it?" I asked the question Emil chirped in my ear.

Urien pursed his lips. "Fixing the water supply isn't the main problem. I can procure the elements easy enough. It's that everyone's been infected already."

"What can we do? Should we send word to the duchess?" Montel asked, leaning in to make sure he heard every word of the elite behind-the-scenes conversation.

"It's too late for that now. Unless she's riding into our territory this very moment, there's nothing she can do." Urien's eyes cut to me. "It's to you, Rosalie."

I quirked my eyebrow. "Um, okay. Done. What do you need me to do? You know I'll help however I can."

"One of the ingredients in the cure is a portion of a kingly spirit. I can provide that easily enough. The other is the touch of a queen. That's where you come in."

I held up my hands. "Hold up there, chief. You're giving up part of your spirit? How does that even work? And don't you like, need your spirit?"

"There's a spell for it. It's simple enough. It just makes me sleepy, so I go into a deep slumber until my spirit restores itself."

I shook my head as I spoke, unwilling to let this kind of

talk go on any longer. "Not on your life, pal. I mean it. We just got you to wake up. No way are you going to sacrifice yourself like that."

My dad's hand found my shoulder and gripped it to reassure me. "You don't need to worry about me, darling. I'll wake up. Sleep is to restore our magic. That's all this is. I'll give away a portion of my magic, and then it'll return to me once my body regenerates its resources."

I hadn't stopped shaking my head the entire time. "I just got you back. Not happening. I'll do it. You guys can use my magic. That's no sweat to me."

Urien pulled me in for a hug. "Thank you for the offer, but it must be a king. Even if you could do it, I wouldn't allow it any more than you'd permit me to sacrifice myself."

"Then it's settled; you won't do it." I pressed my cheek to his solid chest. "I won't allow it."

"Ah, but that's where you're forgetting that I'm your father. Add being a king to that, and you'll realize that I belong to the people. I'm their biggest servant if I'm to be their greatest ruler. This is what's required of me to assist them how they most need it now, so this is what I shall do."

Draper shook his head. "I'll do it. Rosie's right. It shouldn't be you. Your magic is still coming back. Mine's at full stock. I might only need a short nap to recover."

Urien pulled Draper in with his other arm, holding us both and pressing a kiss to our foreheads. "No more would I permit you to sacrifice yourself, Son. That's the thing about fathers. Dads get to do the sacrificing, so that you can live and play." He squeezed us tight, and I could feel the love he kept on tap for us swelling up and broadening his chest. "I wish nothing more than a lifetime of play for you both."

Bastien turned to Montel, and rattled off a list of ingredients that were totally foreign to me. Then he turned to Urien. "Is there anything else we need for the spell?"

"You forgot virgin blood, but I can tell you've studied extensively. Well done, Bastien."

I knew Judah would chuckle at that last ingredient. "Wouldn't be a legit potion without virgin blood. That's like, Fantasy Fiction 101."

Montel slapped Draper's hand. "I'll bring it all back. Might take me some time to find a virgin who will let me take her blood, but the other things are easy enough to find."

Urien nodded. "Search them out in secret, if you can. We don't want our tormentor to know that we're already on the way to solving it all."

I held up my hand. "You can use my blood. Sounds like a better plan than terrifying someone out there, who's already scared."

Urien and Draper looked over at me with wide eyes. Urien broke out into a proud beam, letting us go so he could bring Bastien into his strong embrace. "Thank you, Son."

No matter how Untouchable he was, I could tell being

hugged by the King of Avalon was a privilege Bastien hadn't been expecting. "Um, thank you, your majesty." When the hug ended, I could tell Bastien was trying to stifle just how shaken he was at the fatherly affection he'd assumed he never needed. He cleared his throat, and then jerked his head toward the hallway. "I'll take Rosie upstairs to get her blood. Draper, you want to help me?" He pointed to Urien. "The spirit's the last part, so don't do the spell on yourself until we actually have all the ingredients and they're all mixed."

"Of course. I'll wait in my chambers."

Bastien walked Montel into the hallway, whispering something before he came back in. Bastien curled his arm around my waist, his palm finding the small of my back, which I knew was a spot on my body he coveted. "Into your room, Ro. Let's go, Draper."

15

A KINGLY SPIRIT

We moved up the steps silently, though I could tell Draper was steaming. When my door shut, he burst out with, "I can't believe how stubborn that man is! Well, I guess I should've, since he's your father, and you're as stubborn as they come. He can't be allowed to sacrifice his spirit so soon after coming back to life. It's too dangerous!"

Bastien latched my bedroom door. "I agree. That's why we're going to do it without him. Montel's going to bring the ingredients up here. We'll have Rosie's blood already, and Draper, we should definitely use your spirit. You're younger than Urien, and you weren't just in a coma for twenty-one years."

Relief washed over Draper. "Finally. Someone who's making some sense. Yes. I'll do it."

Bastien drew his dagger and moved toward the bed,

motioning for me to sit down. "Whoever's behind this is expecting Urien to sacrifice himself. He knows what the cure is, and that Urien would do anything to save his people. I'd be willing to bet anything that he's waiting for the king to be incapacitated before he makes his next move. I say we don't let him get that far."

I chewed on my lower lip. "But I don't want Draper to get hurt, either. Giving up part of your spirit? I mean, isn't that kind of terrible?"

Draper waved off my concern. "Pfft. It's nothing. It'll put me to sleep, is all. So long as my body's safe, I'm fine with that." His eyes darted to Bastien. "Can you make sure someone stays with my body?"

I scooped up his hand. "I won't leave your side."

Draper pecked my cheek. "Yes, you will. You'll have to. You're the 'touch of a queen' that's needed to administer the cure to the people. You'll have to leave me, and you'd better, or the people will die, and I'll have given up my spirit for nothing."

I let Draper wrap his arm around my back as he sat down on the bed at my side. "Okay, someone actually explain all this craziness to me. None of this makes much sense."

Draper squeezed my bicep and then rubbed slowly up and down my arm as he spoke. "The potion with the spirit, the virgin blood and all of it is to redeem the wells. To make sure there's a fresh water source available to us. But we're still all infected, so we need a separate cure for that.

It's two separate antidotes for the two parts of the problem. A touch of a queen with a *guérison* elixir will cure the people."

"Dude, I don't know what a *guérison* elixir is. And I'm not exactly a queen."

Bastien shrugged, standing before us in the lamplight. "Draper's not exactly a king, but royalty is in his blood, so it'll work. You've got a queen in your blood, so you can heal them."

"Huh?" My nose crinkled.

Bastien's business expression melted into a soft smile. "I like your confused face. This probably isn't the time, but it's really cute."

I crossed my eyes just to be goofy, idly wondering if he would've still pursued me this hard if I was still under Lane's concealment charm. "Am I cute like this?"

"Adorable. We'll make the *guérison* elixir. It's basically purified honey, *sain* beetroots, and a fennel and watercress tisane, which are all things we have in the kitchen. Then you'll need to dip your finger into the bowl and touch it to the tongue of everyone in the land."

My mouth fell open. "I'm touching everyone's tongues? Isn't that kind of unsanitary?"

Draper shifted next to me. "Better than them all dying. They ache for the chance to be near you, even if you didn't have the cure."

My eyebrows pushed together, but I nodded. "Okay. It's weird, but that's fine. I can do that."

Bastien turned his focus to Draper. "Good. Now that we're all on the same page, I want you to go down to the kitchen and start preparing the *guérison* elixir. Let's move on this as quickly as possible."

"On it." Draper kissed my temple before he stood. "I love you, you know. It'll all be fine."

I gazed up at him, wondering how I'd lived for so long without his brotherly affection. "I don't like the idea of someone taking your spirit. I love your spirit."

Draper grinned at me. "And you'll have it back soon enough. Really, I have the easy job. You're the one who has to explain what we did to Urien when he finds out. I'm guessing he won't be too pleased."

I grimaced. "Right. Yikes. Want to trade?"

"Nope. Think I'll enjoy my nap and let you deal with the fallout. Be back in a few."

After Draper left, Bastien retrieved the large ceramic bowl from my stand behind the partition where I bathed. Then my *Guardien* knelt in front of me, his dagger glinting in the lantern's light. The soft feather-like flickers against his skin made him look impossibly more breathtaking than I remembered. I was so glad he'd shaved off his beard, and was back to his perpetual five o'clock shadow. "Okay, let's get your blood, then. We don't need a ton, but enough to cover the bottom of this basin. You up for it?"

I couldn't help myself as I leaned forward, cupping his face with my hands. There were so many things that were wrong with us, but they took a backseat when my heart remembered all the things I adored about the man I probably should never have loved. "You found a way to save my dad. Thank you."

"Your family *is* you. I know you," he replied simply.

I probably shouldn't have kissed him, but his eyes gazed into mine with such a gentle devotion that I couldn't hold myself back any longer. I closed the gap between us and stroked my lips against his, tasting the cinnamon flavor I'd been missing.

Kissing Bastien felt like a fresh breath my soul had been suffocating without. I sank off the bed into his arms that reeled me in, straddling his lap as he rocked back to sit on his butt. His hands were trembling as they slid up my sides, gripping and caressing with pressure he kept switching from light to punishing. I could tell he wanted to ravish me, but was holding himself back to let me control the pace and passion of our reunion.

His lashes flew open when I pushed him backward, pressing his shoulders to the rug so I could dominate the powerful beast I loved. Bastien let me win, submitting to my lips as if they were his most beloved master. I rewarded his eagerness to let me lead with slow and luscious kisses. They felt like music, and sounded like the sweetest song. My legs straddling him permitted my hips to move slowly back and forth with the beat only we heard. Suddenly our bodies were a symphony of something beautiful that couldn't be quantified as he undulated against me.

"I love you," I whispered against his lips.

Bastien let out a strangled noise that sounded like both pleasure and anguish. "I've loved you for so long. I'll never screw this up again."

I kissed him, my body sliding against his as we made up without the use of any more words.

16

MY BLOOD LOSS, HIS PAIN

I suppose I should've been grateful that Montel hurried back with the ingredients we needed, but my face was borderline resentful as I rolled off of Bastien to open the door to let Montel inside. "Hey, man. Wow. That was fast."

"I kept everything done in secret, just as you asked."

I tried to be decent at hiding our romp on the rug, but Bastien wasn't so covert. He combed his fingers through his hair and moved toward me like a magnet, his lips caressing the back of my neck when he drew my spine to his chest. It was a clear declaration of "Look what I've got," and it wasn't lost on Montel, who gasped.

"But I thought your engagement to Madigan the Formidable would be back on the table." Montel glanced over his shoulder, moved into my bedroom and shut the door behind him. "For your own safety, you might want to keep this affair secret, Princess. The Éirish Untouchables aren't known to be particularly forgiving."

I shirked out of Bastien's embrace and shot him a "be cool" look that he clearly couldn't have cared less about. Bastien was beaming, his grin stretching from ear to ear. "It's fine, Montel, but thanks for looking out. Mad knows all about Bastien and me, and he's more than happy about it. Mad was only going to marry me to save me from being handed over to Duke Henri."

Montel's mouth fell open as he recalculated the new information into his view of the girl who'd worked by his side day after day for two months now. "Oh. Wow. I guess that changes things a bit. Well done, both of you."

Bastien moved in to kiss me in front of Montel, but I skirted his advance. "Hey, now. Not in front of people. That's gross."

Bastien surprised me by fisting the front of my shirt and jerking me forward so that my lips were mere inches from his. "I've got half a mind to take you out into the Town Square and roll around with you up on that platform, so everyone knows that *I'm* the one in your bed every night. I've waited too long for this, Daisy."

I gaped at him, his heady words hitting me like a truck from out of nowhere. "Well, you're going to have to tuck that away for the viewers. My personal life shouldn't be town gossip."

He tugged me up so I was on my tiptoes, and then

pressed his cheek to mine so he could whisper in my ear, "Let them talk. Let them all know that I'm yours."

His words sent a shiver up my spine. He'd gone from not being able to be too near me in public to wanting to mount me in the middle of Town Square. It was a swift shift, and I wasn't sure what to do with the whiplash. "This is what you want? You're sure?"

"Give me half an hour more, and you'll never have to question my loyalties ever again." Bastien's eyes blazed with a fire I was all too familiar with. I knew he was a breath from laying one on me in front of Montel.

I ducked out of his grip and held up my hands before everything tumbled further out of control. "Okay, we'll talk later. But you can't go telling people we're together. We haven't even discussed that yet."

Bastien took a step back, reeling as if I'd slapped him. "What are you talking about? What more is there to discuss?"

I shook my head. "It's not as easy as kissing, Bastien. You know there's too much between us to get off that easily." I sniggered at my phrasing, unable to help myself. "'Get off.' I'm funny."

"Are you serious?" He shook his head, and then crossed his arms over his chest. "Fine. Let's talk."

"Um, hello. We have company and a job to do. We can talk later."

"We can talk now! I'm tired of being apart, Daisy. I

mean it. What do we need to sort out? Let's do it right here, right now."

Montel ducked his head and tried to leave, but Bastien held up his hand to tell Montel that no one was going anywhere until this was sussed out.

I buried my face in my hands. "Dude, talk to Lane or my dad. I want to be with you, but I'm all turned around from when you split. I don't know that I can trust us yet, especially not enough to be so serious so quick. If you want to be with me, talk to either one of my parents. Make your case to them why we should be together. If you can convince someone you can't kiss into a puddle that we should be together, then I'm in."

Bastien guffawed. "You can't be serious."

"Oh, I'm deadly serious. If Lane was here, I'd send you to her, but Urien will work, too. My dad wouldn't let me do something stupid. So if being with you is stupid, he'll put a stop to it. If getting back with you is the smart thing to do, then he'll be able to see that. I can't see clearly anymore, Bastien. If you want to be with me, then this is how to move forward."

Bastien nodded, though I could tell he didn't love this prospect. "Done. I'll go right now."

I pressed my palm to the door to stop him. "No. The kingdom's more important than us getting back together. Antidote first." I shook my head at myself, embarrassed that this was all out in the open for my work friend to read into and form opinions on. "Sorry, Montel. Totally inappropriate and uncool of us. Let's do this cure thing. That's the big deal we should be focused on, not who's kissing whom."

Montel quirked his eyebrow at me with a dubious tilt of his head. "Virgin blood? Are you quite sure you can provide that? Because we can't skimp on any of these ingredients. They all have to be accurate."

I held up my hand, like I was swearing the weirdest oath I'd ever needed to prove. "Honest. Chastity belt firmly in place." Then, because I was a dork with a crude sense of humor, I added. "I'm a vegetarian anyway, so definitely no porking for me."

Montel's smile was colored with embarrassment at my locker room joke. "Yes, well. I've got everything except the king's spirit and the virgin blood."

Bastien sat me down on the side of the bed, again taking the same kneeling position in front of me that had gotten us into so much trouble to begin with. He glanced up at me with a secretive smile, and I knew he was picturing our heated kiss that was still burning through our bodies. His dagger glinted in the flickering lamplight, the flames reflecting off the metal like tiny interpretive dancers that twisted and writhed for Bastien. He certainly knew how to make a girl writhe. He met my gaze with a determined one that told me to buck up, and then pressed the point to my forearm, but didn't pierce me. I could tell he was struggling, wanting to do the right thing, but feeling all wrong about it. Finally, he withdrew the knife. "I can't do it. I don't know why, but I can't make myself cut you. It feels all off."

"It's that pesky love stuff." I took the knife from him while Montel held the empty basin beneath my elbow. "It's cool. I've got this." I hesitated only for the amount of time it took me to suck in a deep breath, then I let the dagger sting me. The cut wasn't harrowingly deep, but I hissed at the sting as it rippled through my arm. The red began to pool and drip, sliding over my forearm and dribbling down my elbow into the bowl. "How much?"

Montel answered for Bastien, who I could tell didn't like the sight of my blood. "More than this. I don't think that cut went deep enough."

I worked the slice open further, grimacing at the freefall of the blood into the bowl. I shut my eyes like a chicken, but the guys didn't call me on it. My blood was literally spilling for Avalon. I bled for the place I'd been trying to leave from the beginning. I was far off the mark from where I'd wanted to be at this point, and yet, here I was. My eyes met Bastien's with unconcealed sadness. "I was supposed to be a veterinarian. I was going to graduate college by now."

Bastien's hand cuffed the nape of my neck, and he brought his forehead to rest against mine. "Hey, you can still have all that. When we go to your world, you'll get right back into school, and you'll graduate."

My heart lurched, though that was partly because of Bastien's pledge, and partly because my heart had to pump overtime to keep up with the blood loss. "You said 'we'. Did you mean it?"

Bastien's gaze said far more than anything else could, but still he tried to put words to the promise he kissed into my lips. "I would follow you to the ends of whatever world we land in."

Montel's voice reluctantly broke through our reverie. "Surely you wouldn't abandon your people, Princess."

I straightened, turning to meet Montel's concerned brown eyes. "I already did abandon my people to come here. My people are the Commoners. I ditched my best friend, my education and my life to help out Avalon. I'll stay as long as I need to, but then I'm going home."

"You'll want to keep that to yourself, Montel," Bastien warned. "Rosie won't leave before Avalon's ready for her to step aside."

Montel squeezed my arm, milking the blood so it flowed through its waning vigor. "Avalon would not be the same. We left our homes to come back to Province 9 because we wanted to serve you and the Duchess. You were the one we rallied around. If you left us to fend off Morgan by ourselves? I can't imagine the home we're fighting to save right now with this very blood would last long."

I swallowed, unsure what to say to this. "That's sweet, Montel. But I think you all are stronger than one person. I'm just a regular girl, nothing more. It's the crown that gets people confused."

Montel's eyes hardened. "You're not just a girl. You're a symbol for all that was broken in us. When we saw you being carried out from the well by an Untouchable, it was we who were also being carried over the bumps and pitfalls we hadn't been able to rise up and conquer. We were able to escape Morgan because you did. Suddenly we had our duchess back, and our Avalon Rose. We had Untouchables fighting for us. We had something to live for." Montel shook his head, flabbergasted that I didn't understand all of this. "You're beloved by Master Kerdik, and that is no small thing. You could have easily laid around and feasted your days away in this castle, and we still would have adored you. Instead you chose to work with us, serving the people by being one of the people. You put aside your fancy dresses and got your hands dirty with us, building that wall to keep your people safe. Every time we look at our border, we'll remember that the Avalon Rose is protecting us."

"Well, what else was I supposed to do? You're saying all these things that sound impressive, but they're really pretty normal. You're wowed that Kerdik's my friend? Well, there have been times where Kerdik was my only friend. Loser Rosie had one whole friend. Super impressive. And we bicker more than anything else." My eyelids started to droop. "And I wasn't about to let everyone else do all the work while I laid around eating bonbons all day long. Boring."

The corners of Montel's mouth lifted. "That's precisely

what I mean. If you left, that unbreakable spirit you rallied in us might be lost."

My fingers were stiff and cold, but I was afraid to look in the basin to see if there was enough. "Are we good yet? Do we still need more blood? I'm starting to fade, here."

"Just a little more," Montel urged, squeezing my arm again as he held my wrist over the bowl.

Bastien pressed his face into my neck and let out a quiet whine of distress. I tried to comb my fingers through his hair, but my hand was so clumsy, I only managed to swat at the back of his head before my arm flopped over his shoulder. "What's wrong, honey?"

"It's taking too long! I don't like that we're using your blood. Why couldn't we have just found a maiden from the village?"

I tried to comfort Bastien, but it seemed my blood loss was causing him the most pain. "Hey, it's alright. How many times have you been banged up? And yet, you survived. This is just a little cut. Probably won't even leave much of a scar."

Bastien pressed a kiss into the crook of my neck, but instead of making me swoon in the deliciously good way, my eyes rolled back and I passed right the crap out in the middle of my bedroom.

17

ALWAYS MY BROTHER

I awoke to Bastien frantically slapping my cheek and calling my name. I gazed up at him from my spot on the floor, curious as to how I ended up on the rug to begin with. Montel had my arm in his hands, bandaging while I was still limp and useless. "What happened?"

"We took too much blood!" Bastien shouted, angry at Montel.

My buddy tried not to be intimidated, and instead focused on the job at hand. "It wasn't too much. It was the right amount, unless you want her to have to go through all of this again when it doesn't work because we babied her. She's alright. She's not a shrinking violet. The Avalon Rose builds walls and commands countries. She's strong enough to weather a small cut. It's a little blood loss, which she was completely up for. We didn't even extract any of her magic in the process. This will be easy to heal from."

I clumsily batted at Bastien's cheek, but then my hand lost its oomph and slammed down across my face.

"Is that what you meant to do?" Bastien asked with a patience he didn't have for Montel. He moved my hand off my face and kissed feeling back into it, his prickly scruff chafing the skin.

"You're so hairy," I warbled.

Bastien sniggered. "That's how you like me, I'm pretty sure."

"I do."

Bastien waited until Montel tied off the bandage, and then hoisted me up in his arms. He rested me gently on the mattress just as Draper let himself in to the bedroom, giving us a thumbs-up with one hand while holding a large, lidded bowl with the other. "Everything's all set for the Queen's touch antidote." He set the covered bowl down on the nightstand and moved closer to get a better look at my face. His eyebrows pushed together in concern he didn't bother tempering. "Rosie! What happened to you? How much blood did they take? You're white as a sheet!"

Montel rolled his eyes, exasperated at having to defend himself again. "I already told Bastien, she's okay. We took what we needed. She's a little thing, so of course it laid her out. She knew what she was getting into, and she's fine with it. Our princess is no scared child."

Draper didn't pay Montel any attention, but moved to

the bedside and smoothed my hair back from my damp forehead. "Baby Rosie, are you alright?"

I managed a small smile up at him. "I'm alright, and it's been decades since I was a baby. You worry too much, big brother."

"Ah, don't you know? Worrying's what I do when it comes to you. You'll always be my Baby Rosie, no matter how old you get."

My vision swam, and suddenly there were two of him. "How'd I get so lucky?"

Draper kissed my forehead before he turned to Bastien and Montel. "Is everything else ready? Are we just waiting on my spirit?"

Bastien straightened and moved over to the basin of blood. "Give me a couple minutes to make sure it's all in place. Take your time and do what you need, because when it's time to use your spirit, we have a small window."

Draper nodded, and I expected him to start performing some kind of hocus pocus ninja action to ready his spirit for... whatever it was supposed to do. Instead he laid his head down on the pillow by my side and pulled me into his arms so that my head rested in the nook of his outstretched arm. His lips pressed to my bandage with a small grin. "Just like when you were a baby. If you bumped yourself when you were learning to crawl or walk, I was the one with the magic in my kiss that healed you."

I glanced down at my bandaged arm. "Well, would you look at that? I'm all better. Must be magic."

His arms tightened around me, and his smile vanished. "I want you to listen to me, Rosie. Listen close, okay?"

"What's wrong? You look upset."

Draper's voice quieted to a whisper. "If anything happens to me, I have a small fortune buried in the Lost Village. It's behind my old place of business, buried deep thirty paces south of the tallest tree."

My eyes widened. "Why are you telling me this? You're going to be fine, right?"

"Of course I am. Now, listen. If something should happen to me, I want you to dig up the money and keep it." He swallowed hard and looked deep into my eyes. "Don't forget me, Pumpkin."

My eyes wetted with emotion I didn't want to deal with right now. "Drape, stop it. You said you're going to be fine. Why are you talking like this?"

He ignored my question and rolled on his side so we could snuggle nose to nose. He brought my hand up between us so he could kiss my fingertips. "I have letters I wrote you all in my desk. Make sure you, Lane, Urien, Gwen and Damond get them and read them after I'm gone."

It was then I saw the fear plain in his eyes. Whatever we were about to do was dangerous, and Draper was very much afraid of the fallout. "No. You'll deliver the letters yourself when you wake up."

He held my hand to his cheek as his dark lashes fluttered shut. Even though he was far older than me, he looked like a scared little boy. "Tell Lane that I was lost without her, and that she's always been the mother I needed. Tell her I love her, and that I don't want her to be sad."

I tried to sit up, but my body was still too weak. "Bastien! Bastien, what are we about to do? Draper's talking like he's never going to wake up, but that's not true, right?"

Bastien's closed expression when he turned around didn't give me much hope. "Of course not. Draper's going to be fine. He might sleep for longer than he's comfortable with, but he'll wake up. I was scared my first time, too." His eyes met Draper's. "Your spirit's going to regenerate, brother. Sleeping isn't as bad as you're thinking."

"Of course it's not bad! Draper, are you afraid to sleep?"

Draper nodded, anguish pulling his features downward. "Urien slept for twenty-one years when Morgan stole part of his spirit."

"I thought Morgan poisoned Dad! What are you talking about?"

"To weaken him, she stole part of his spirit. Then the poison sealed his fate. He couldn't recover because the poison blocked his spirit from regenerating. That's why I can't let Urien do this. I know whoever did this to our land is counting on Urien forfeiting his own spirit to the cause. I know they're counting on him to weaken himself so they can slip more Hemlock to him and keep him under." He blinked away tears that I could tell embarrassed him. "Don't let anyone do that to me!"

I flung a clumsy arm around my brother. "Draper, no! Honey, we won't let anyone near your body. No one's gunning for you. They won't even know it was you who donated your spirit."

Bastien nodded. "We'll keep Urien locked in the castle, so the cloaked idiot, or whoever's behind this, thinks he's weakened. That'll make sure no one targets you. Plus, I'll post Link in here with you. He won't let anything past that solid door, you hear?"

Draper let himself indulge in a few muted shudders before he nodded. "Okay. Yeah. If Urien's hidden, that's best. Thanks, Bastien." His chest moved unevenly, and I could tell he was still freaking out. "Watch her for me. I mean, more closely than any other assignment you were given throughout your whole career. I don't care that Avalon needs Rosie; *I* need my sister. I lost her once, Bastien. You can't begin to understand what that was like. I won't go through that again."

I combed my clumsy fingers through Draper's black hair, kissing his forehead and shushing his worries so he didn't have a full-blown panic attack. "Honey, honey. It's alright. I'm not going anywhere. I promise. I love you. I'll be so super safe. I'll be boring. It sounds like I'm not doing anything except letting an entire province suck on my finger for the next day or so." My nose crinkled at the visual I still hadn't made peace with. "I'll keep Bastien with me the entire time."

Draper nodded with his eyes squinched tight. He held onto me with the desperation of a child seeking out comfort from his mother. Draper had been alone for so long; it was unrealistic to expect he'd escape a heavy dose of neurosis. He held onto me, holding me around the waist while I stroked his hair, his cheek, his arm. When he finally spoke again, it came out a pained whisper. "Know that I love you, and I always have. You were more precious to me than my own sister. Try as I did to be a good brother to Gwen when she was adopted into our family, she dismissed me the second Duke Henri did. That adoring look in your eyes when you greet me? Don't ever let that fade. I need that. I need to be the hero in someone's eyes, instead of always being the villain or the waste."

My expression darkened as Bastien and Montel came near us with the bowl, wearing grave looks of their own. "You listen to me, Draper. You are not a villain, and you've never been a waste. A girl needs her big brother, so you'd better not take more than a half hour cat nap. I mean it. I'll come up here and lay the smack down if you just lie around here all day and keep me waiting." I frowned at him. "And don't think that because you needed a nap means that you get out of helping out around here. That wall still needs building, mister."

Draper managed a slight chuckle. "You're strict."

"I love you." I didn't know how else to comfort him, so I

went back to a childhood I couldn't remember, and pulled out the song he'd made up to sing to me when I'd been young and inconsolable. "'Climb all the mountains, run off when you're grown, but for now, little boy, my song is your home.'"

He reached over and stroked my cheek, fondling a curl that called out to him. "Always my sister."

I nodded once, and then swiped at one of his tears with my thumb. "Always my brother."

18

LOOSE LADIES LOVE LINK

"I've never in all my years thought my daughter would grow up to disregard my wishes completely. I was perfectly clear, was I not? I told you both that we would use my spirit, but you went ahead and did what you thought was best, ignoring the fact that I know the dangers far better than you."

It was minute ten of my dad's tirade, and I'm not sure what amused me more – that we'd broken through the polite getting-to-know-you stage of our relationship with all his yelling, or that Bastien and I had actually pulled it off. "I feel like you're hungry. Bastien gets crabby when he's hungry, too. You want me to go grab you something from the kitchen?"

This only steamed Urien's grits more. "I'm not 'crabby', child, I'm outraged!"

"Hulk, smash!" I roared, pounding my fists on the table. I pointed to his face as I turned to Bastien. "Do my eyebrows look like that when I get pissed? I don't know how you resist me. It's totally adorable."

Bastien sniggered, but had the decency to cover his mouth and turn his head in an attempt to conceal the disrespect I was determined to get away with. He cleared his throat when Urien's nostrils flared. "Apologies, your majesty. We only used Draper's spirit because yours is still on the mend. The three of us were afraid you would fall back into a deeper sleep than we could pull you out of." Before my dad could rage some more, Bastien added, "Plus, using your spirit is exactly what whoever poisoned the wells would expect us to do. I'm sure he's just waiting for you to be incapacitated so he can make his next move. Your kingdom needs you."

Dad's head bowed, his chin moving from side to side in frustration. "That was not for you to decide. You sacrificed my son on a mere assumption."

I was sitting with my legs crossed atop the marble coffee table in the study. All the rooms seemed oddly long – rectangular instead of square. I was tossing a tennis ball-sized rock I'd found from one palm to the other, chuckling to myself about how easy it was to get my dad's goat. It was fun getting to know him, testing his temper to see how far it would bend until he devolved back into the puppy I adored.

Yeah, I might have some issues with authority.

Bastien puffed out his chest like a soldier and fashioned his hands to the small of his back. "Draper wouldn't hear of you sacrificing yourself. Either way, it's done. You can take out your anger on me, sir. It was my idea."

"And a foolish one, indeed. Well done, taking the blame. You know I can't very well throw an Untouchable in the dungeon."

"I'll go if you send me. I have no problem bowing to your authority." Bastien quirked an eyebrow at my dad when he added, "When you're not suicidal, that is."

Urien clenched his jaw. "I wasn't going to die."

"All due respect, but Rosie deserves to have as big a family as she can get. I won't let anyone take away something good from the princess, not even you. Draper will heal far easier."

I caught Bastien's eye and smiled, tossing him the rock so we could play catch. "You love me. I see it."

Bastien was enjoying our reunion, especially the fact that it was all on display for my father. "You know I do." His churlish grin had a touch of bashfulness to it. He was declaring himself to my dad, as well as defying the king in the same breath. It made us both a little giddy.

Dad was not amused. Or at least he wanted us to think he wasn't amused. Either way, he wore a frown of deep displeasure, his arms crossed over his broad chest. "Link is watching over Draper's body?"

"Of course. And the magical goodness potion with my

blood and the spirit and whatnot is on its way to the wells. Montel and Mad are delivering it now. Once they get back, I'll go to the Town Square and start letting people suck on my fingers." I turned my chin toward Bastien. "Oh, can you round up some of the Wildmen? If they can use their panpipes to keep the people calm while they wait in line to get the cure, that would be helpful."

"On it. Great suggestion."

My dad frowned at us. "If only anything in Avalon was easy these days. You two have rendered me completely useless in saving my people."

I caught the rock Bastien tossed me, and then stretched out my arms to him. "I feel like you need a hug. It's gotta be hard when we don't let you get the life sucked outta you. I mean, now you get to, I don't know, bring order to the nation like a chump. Rough break. Come here, buddy."

Dad shook his head at me, though I could tell he was trying not to smile. "You're trying to pass your insubordination off as a joke, and it's not working."

"Yes, it super is." I tossed the rock to him, grinning when he caught it without meaning to participate in the levity. "Not for nothing, but I love you. Sort of getting attached to you being upright. I'll be as insubordinate as it takes to keep you with me. If you don't like it, well, you know, I don't care."

Bastien barked out a laugh that made tears form in the corners of his eyes. It was the best kind of crying on him, and I was glad I got to witness it. When he caught wind of my dad's disapproval, he instantly sobered. "Not funny, Rosie. Not funny at all."

My dad's eyes cut to mine. "I guess I should be used to you making calls like this 'for my own good,' Britney Spears." The reminder of the fake name I'd used made me duck my head with a grimace.

It was the perfect moment for Montel to return, basin empty and a look of accomplishment on his face. "Looks like it's time to round up the locals," I observed. "Everything go alright?"

"Not the slightest hiccup, Princess. Madigan the Formidable sent out riders into the province, summoning everyone to the Town Square."

"That's my cue." I took Bastien's hand and hopped down from the coffee table.

I trotted up the steps and let myself into the bedroom where Link sat, guarding Draper's body. The whole thing was super intense whenever anyone from Avalon slept, so I followed the laws of the land and made sure Draper's nap was a peaceful one, keeping my voice to a whisper when I greeted Link. "I'm just washing up and changing. The well's been cured, so now it's just the people we need to worry about."

"Grand. The sooner it's over, the sooner we can all get back to normal life. Mad and I had such a good rhythm with the men we were whipping into soldiers. I don't want to lose too many nights to this." He glanced at Draper's body warily. "Is he supposed to be this still? The times I've seen ye sleep, ye tossed and turned."

I leaned over the mattress and saw that my brother's chest was still moving up and down. "Yeah, that's just me, though. Not everyone has such a hard time sleeping. So long as he's breathing, he's alright." I slipped behind the partition with a clean dress, and took my work clothes off. I used the rag and the water pitcher to sponge myself off. "Hey, Link?"

"Aye?"

"Thanks for helping out so much. You're not even from Avalon, but you're giving up your time and energy to help get us on track. Super way cool of you."

"Avalon's not your home either, and you're about to go stick your finger into the gobs of a whole province. If we weren't here, what else would we be doing?"

"I dunno. Searching for the pot of gold at the end of the rainbow? Eating Lucky Charms to your heart's content? I honestly don't know what I would've done without you and Mad back to help bring order to the chaos."

"We won't stay forever, but while we're here, we don't mind helping. Plus, we need to stay until we find the man who controlled Mad. Can't have a git like tha running around, or we'll never stop looking over our shoulders."

I splashed a little water on my face, careful not to let any dribble into my mouth. "You love him."

"Aye. I love all my brothers. Some more than others,

sure. Mad and I've been through the most together, though."

"I think you two are precious."

"Jays, woman. Don't go making a song of it."

"How is it I'm one of only two girlfriends of an Untouchable?" I winced that I'd already moved Bastien back into the role of boyfriend in my mind. That one really snuck up on me.

"Why have one lass when ye can have them all?"

"Oh, you charmer." I smiled at Link's brash nature as I toweled off. Then I threw the dress over my head. It was emerald, of course, but it had dusky pink lace embellishments along the hem and the bust. The fitted waist wasn't too tight, but it definitely showed off the fact that I was a woman with an unabashed hourglass figure. The capped sleeves hugged the tops of my shoulders, with silver sheer fabric hanging down the backs of my arms like waterfalls.

"How about ye?" Link asked as I twisted my hair into a bun on the top of my head.

"What about me? I don't need to bag all the lasses in the kingdom."

Link snorted from his chair. "I mean how is it Bastien's your first lad? Seems like Common lads are blind as a bat to let ye slip through their fingers."

I chuckled and came out from behind the partition. "That's sweet. How do I look? Will this fool them into thinking I'm a princess?"

Link grinned salaciously at me as he leaned back in his

chair, not bothering to hold anything from his cheesy leer. I expected nothing less from the goofball. "Aye. It'll fool them into following ye over a cliff, if tha's your fancy."

"Wow. That's some dress." I walked toward the bed to get another look at Draper, standing next to where Link sat.

Link picked up my hand, and gave it a little kiss. "Nah. It's not the dress tha charms them. Tha's just who ye are, Rosie."

I squeezed his fingers in appreciation for his sweetness before my gaze fell to Draper. I bit down on my lower lip, trying not to worry over a silly little nap. It was all their building it up into something harrowing that had me on edge. Link and I entwined our fingers to hold tighter to each other as we watched Draper like the creepers we were. "He'll be fine," I ruled, needing someone to say it out loud. "He promised he would be alright."

"Aye." Link's boots were on the edge of the bed so he could balance his chair on two legs without toppling over. "I'll watch your brother, wee Rose. Go on out and help your people." He squeezed my fingers. "Keep Bastien with ye, though. And if Mad's with ye, remember the magic word in case someone triggers him again."

"Meara," I recalled with certainty. "You think Mad's alright? He's been a little withdrawn since you three came back. I've barely seen him around."

Link chuckled, low and deep. "He's upset tha he attacked ye, for one. And he doesn't know what to do when ye get angry at him. We weren't expecting ye to be hurt tha we left. Mad's not used to caring what a lass thinks."

My head jerked to Link in confusion. "You two don't care what I think."

In a move so swift, I didn't have the forethought to counter it, Link yanked me down so my face was inches from his. "It killed me to go, after ye asked us to stay. Do ye think it's every day we find somewhere we can rest our heads? Do ye think we trust easily? We're alive because we don't trust, don't rest, don't stop. Tha we found ye – a soft beauty to watch over us?" He shook his head at my assumptions, that I was just beginning to understand had been all wrong. He tugged me down to sit on his lap, anchoring all four legs of the chair to the ground. His arm wrapped around my hips, my legs sandwiched loosely between his open thighs. "We sobered up Bastien quick as we could so we could come back to ye."

I blinked at him, shocked at the sincerity I didn't realize he was capable of. I wanted to ask what I did that was so special, but instead I kissed his cheek so I could watch him turn bashful. A smile swept over my lips when I saw the nape of his neck and the tips of his ears turn pink. His scars were covered with zipper tattoos that climbed out of his collar, begging my fingers to trace them. "Thank you for coming back. I love you three knuckleheads."

Link's mouth tugged up on one side. "Love ye, too, wee sister."

I pulled back, straightening and trying to look dignified. "Hello, I'm clearly the older sibling. I'm way more responsible than you are. You get to be the wee brother, if anything."

"I'm older, so I get to be the strapping big brother." His gaze went back to Draper as he wrapped his arms around me and rested his chin atop my shoulder. "Ye never let me get away with anything, even though I've got this handsome mug." He jerked his thumb to his face.

"Yes, you're very pretty. All the loose ladies love Link. Now, be a good boy, sweetie. I'll be back when it's all done."

"I'll be a boy, but tha's the most I can do for ye." He turned my wrist and pushed his thumb into the heel of my hand, so that my fingers opened up to him. He pressed a kiss to the center of my palm, then smirked up at me like the cutie pie he would never stop being. "My mammy used to do tha before I went to school for the day. Keeps the love with ye all day long."

I balled my hand into a fist, my heart swelling at the tenderness Link didn't often like to wave around. "Then I'll be sure not to drop it. And that's probably the most precious thing in the universe. When you do find a real girl worth settling down for, try that adorableness on her. She'll swoon to the moon for you." I lifted his larger hand and kissed the well of his palm with a small smile. "In case you run low on love while I'm gone."

Link blinked at his hand, and I could see a million flickers of nostalgia and emotion sweeping across his usually foolhardy features. I wondered how long it had been since he'd seen his mother – if she was even still alive. "Aye." He swallowed hard, and then tried to shake off the tender moment by rubbing the kiss all over his face and scrubbing it under his armpits.

I grinned at his silliness, and blew him another kiss, which he caught and tucked into his pocket like the cutie pie he was. I pecked Draper's cheek and left, readying to face the nation.

19

STRANGERS SUCKING ON MY FINGERS

It didn't take long for Mad's men to send word through the region to meet in the Town Square for the cure. The people clambered to the platform where I'd been given a chair to sit on (and by chair, I mean a fancy mini throne that made me feel like a tool). Bastien stood on my left, and Mad was at my right, with Montel and a few guys organizing everyone into a line while reminding them to be patient. The Wildmen did their part, playing pleasant songs on their panpipes that relaxed the people and kept them from growing restless while they waited in line for the cure.

I don't know why I chose this moment to revert back into an introvert, but I found myself too shy to speak when the whole region had their eyes on me. The wooden bowl was on my lap, so I sat perfectly still, hoping the honey mixture wouldn't spill.

Bastien seemed to sense my discomfort, and made the announcement that everyone would get their medicine, and that no one would be turned away from receiving the cure if they were patient. He also announced that the wells were pure again, and safe for drinking, but to dump out any other water in pitchers or tubs or whatever that had been collected before tonight. The ravens gathered around the platform eighty strong, cheeping out Bastien's message, in case anyone was uncertain that they enforced our rule. I kind of loved them for the sweet songs they sang me.

When the first person came forward, it was an elderly man and his grandson. They both opened their mouths wide and stuck their tongues out at me after they bowed. I glanced up at Bastien, nervous we'd made it this far, and I would screw it all up in the ninth inning. "Just dip my finger into the honey and touch it to their tongues?"

Bastien nodded. "Quick as you can. Montel's got everyone in order for now, but you never know how long it'll last."

Mad glared at the old man. "Is this your kid? Fess up, now." He motioned to the meek Annabelle, who was sitting on the platform, clinging to his calf. No one had claimed her, but he was determined to get to the bottom of it all today. She seemed perfectly content to sit at his feet, not worried in the least that no one had come to find her all night long. She had a long scar that stretched from her temple all the way down to her chin; it looked like a mark from the crack of a whip or something terrible.

"No, Madigan the Formidable. I've never seen her before." The old man and the boy dipped their heads to me after I brushed my finger to their bumpy tongues, curing them with a simple touch. It felt like cheating somehow. I thought about all the intricacies our scientists and doctors had to study and manipulate to come up with cures and vaccinations. To just touch an herbed honey to their tongues felt too easy (albeit, totally gross).

The sun was just starting to rise, highlighting the worry on everyone's faces as the line slowly moved forward. One by one, we worked our way through the people, with Aimee and Pascal taking everyone's names and new addresses down, along with their former region and their occupation. That was one of the ideas I came up with on the fly. I didn't know if a census was super important, but so many new people had immigrated into the region, I guessed it would be a good idea to get a solid count so we knew what we were dealing with.

The line seemed to stretch on forever, never getting any smaller. To their credit, the people were patient, dealing with fussy babies and the boredom of standing in one place for too long with grace I hadn't expected.

I tried to stifle a yawn a few hours into the job, but Bastien noticed. "You're about ten percent of the way through the line, as far as I can tell. You're doing great."

I'd pulled an all-nighter, minus the few minutes the blood loss had knocked me out. I was starting to feel the exhaustion, and wondered how many days I could be expected to power through.

When the sun rose overhead, alerting me that it was nearing noon, Montel brought me a roll with some sort of nutty spread on it. I munched on it with one hand, while my other finger kept dipping and swiping, dipping and swiping. I did my best to keep a bland smile on my face, but by the time the afternoon hit, I knew I looked a breath from passing out. "Emil, could you and your friends go scout out the perimeter? I could use the backup." The bird who'd been my faithful companion all morning chirped his happiness to comply and rallied his troops. I sighed with relief once they all flew out.

"You worried about the border?" Bastien inquired as he watched Emil fly away.

"Not particularly. But if I keep using my magic to listen to the birds, you're going to have to carry me out of here."

"I wouldn't mind that one bit. My damsel in distress for everyone to see in my arms."

I shot him a look to be cool as I dipped my disgusting finger back into the bowl of herbed honey. "We aren't talking about that here."

"Where are we having that discussion? When?"

I sighed, shifting atop my hard mini-throne. My back was stiff from sitting for so long. "After the drama dies down, and I have twenty whole minutes of peace to rub together so I can actually give it some real thought."

Mad was pissed that no one had claimed Annabelle

yet. "Do ye know this wee lass? Tell me the truth, now." He pointed his thick finger in accusation at the couple who was in line next.

They looked like they might simultaneously pee themselves, so I waved Mad's frustration off. "It's fine. We'll find her parents, Mad. Be patient."

"Tha's easy for ye to say. Ye aren't the one with a child clinging to your leg." He glared down at Annabelle. "Are ye still hungry?"

She gazed up at him, her pale grey-blue eyes shining up as her black hair fell away from her face. "Aye, Papa." She was clearly of Avalon's dialect, but she'd picked up on Mad's brogue, trying to make it her own. It was totally precious, and I had to fight hard not to giggle.

Madigan's nostrils flared with barely contained fury that she'd both adopted his language, and that she assumed he'd somehow adopted her. His head whipped to stare at me, as if this was all my fault. "What am I supposed to do with her now? Can't we send her off? She'll find her way to her home."

I guffawed as I continued to stick my finger in people's mouths. "Nice try. You can't send a kid off on their own in a land they're not familiar with. The province is new to everyone. Even the adults are still trying to find their way around the place." I craned my head to smile at her. "Annabelle, do you want another roll?"

She was still warming up to me, and nodded tentatively. I could tell she was ravenous, but was reluctant to relinquish her hold on her new daddy. Mad handed a raisin roll to her from the basket Mercy, Hope and Faith had brought us, but she wouldn't move her hands from Mad's leg. Instead she took bites from the bread as he held it. I could see the affection for Mad, but also the fear of being left alone, exposed to the harshness of life as an orphan. I couldn't understand why her parents hadn't come looking for her. Judging by the patches on her dress that was probably a size too big on her, and the filthiness of her pin-straight hair, she looked like she had been neglected for a while now.

Grateful villagers brought us bowls of stew around dinner, but I didn't take a break to eat mine. I couldn't very well eat stew one-handed with no table to balance the bowl on. "I don't want to stop," I told Aimee when she urged me to eat. "I just want to finish the job." If I craned my neck, I could see the end of the line. It still stretched about three blocks long, but there was an end to it.

Aimee tsked me, as if she was the older one, and I was being young and foolish. "You need to eat something more than bread, your grace."

"I will. I'll eat a whole mastodon after I finish up here."

Bastien and Mad had already finished their bowls. Mad was sitting on the platform next to my throne now, bored of standing in the same spot all friggin' day. "Eat, now," Mad ordered Annabelle, who clung to his arm, disregarding her warm bowl.

"But I..." I could tell she didn't want to let go of him,

and was scared he'd ditch her at the first opportunity. It was anybody's guess if she was wrong or not.

I gave her a tired smile. "Mad won't leave you. I'll make sure he stays right here. You can eat, sweetheart."

Annabelle gazed up at Mad with watery Bambi eyes that could melt even his hard heart. Her whisper was so earnest, it made me want to throw the gross bowl of spit and honey on the floor and scoop her up in my arms. "Please don't leave me, Papa."

Mad's expression hardened, and I hoped he would be gracious. It would be a good time for him to start exhibiting a normal emotional range, instead of that of a corpse or a caveman. "Aye. Eat your supper. And don't look at me like tha. Your Da's out there somewhere. Probably last in line." Then he grumbled. "He'd better be."

Annabelle had the gift of looking past Madigan's grumping and seeing the treasure beneath, as I had. She slowly slid her arm from around his and picked up her bowl, shooting him furtive glances every time he shifted an inch. Though Madigan didn't know all the right words, I watched as he compensated for her fear by sitting perfectly still, so her nerves would be more at ease. It was the equivalent of a hug, and my heart warmed to see him try so hard to be good for her. She wolfed down her bowl, and I could see that though she'd been starving, being abandoned had left a greater vacancy in her than mere hunger ever could.

A shrill series of squawks startled me, sending a zap of

lightning through my tired body. I almost dropped the cure all over the platform. *Run! Run! Peludas are coming for us! Princess, run!*

Bastien's hand was on the hilt of his dagger, though he didn't understand what they said. The urgent tone was clear, though, and he looked to me for verification. "What's wrong?"

"What's a peluda?"

Bastien's eyes widened, and Mad stood abruptly. "Where? In our province?"

I nodded. "They're coming for us. What are they?"

Bastien turned around and punched at the gong. The second the reverberation died down, he shouted, "Everyone into your houses! Take your families and go! Peludas are on their way to the village! The rest of you can get the cure later. I want all the soldiers in training to come forward. We'll need as many swords as we can get."

The Wildmen broke their tune of serenity and started playing a lively ditty that made my heart race, increasing my urge to run home.

My heart pounded as Bastien's warrior-mode face slid into place. I realized with dread as I took in the fearful expressions on the thousands of villagers, that this was the perfect day to plan an ambush on our soil.

20

PORCUPINES ARE HARD TO HUG

I stood, holding the wooden salad bowl on my hip. I didn't know enough about the situation to understand how afraid I should be, so I went with Bastien's level of urgency. My hand was sticky, so I dipped it in the cup of water I was supposed to be drinking while I waited for orders from him. "Bastien, what's a peluda?"

Bastien pinched his nose as he thought. "Not enough time to explain. A giant porcupine who's deadlier than a trained soldier, and we don't exactly have a ton of those hanging around."

"Can't I just talk to them? I mean, if it's an animal, I can help."

Bastien shook his head. "Peludas started out as an animal, but they've been mutated by Morgan le Fae's witchery." He turned to Madigan. "Mad, can you command the men while I run Rosie back to the palace?"

"Aye. Take the wee one with ye, though." He pushed Annabelle toward me, but the poor girl clung to Madigan's arm.

"No, Papa! I'll stay with ye."

I managed a smile for her. "Mad lives at the palace with me. He needs you to pick out a room to stay in while he takes care of a few things out here. He's a total slob, too. Maybe we can surprise him by cleaning up his room for him?" It was a total lie. Mad was a ghost in whatever room he stayed in – the only trace he'd been there was that the room would be cleaner, with everything in right angles. Gotta love him.

She looked up at Mad with a hesitance we just plain didn't have time for. Bastien knelt down to her level and looked her in the eye. "If Mad's your papa, then that makes me your uncle, since Mad's in the Brotherhood with me. Come with Uncle Bastien and Aunt Rosie to the palace, okay? Otherwise things are going to get ugly out here for you."

Mad nodded without any hint of softening when Annabelle looked up at him for guidance. "Go. I'll come back for ye when I'm finished."

She squeezed his arm one more time as the people all around us fled in every direction. Then she placed her hand in mine.

"Leave the bowl, Rosie. We don't have time. They're likely to start setting the place on fire first."

"Huh?" I obeyed, but not before making sure the staff

had all been vaccinated from the well pollution. Then I put my finger in the honey once more, and touched it to Bastien's tongue, then to mine, to Annabelle's, and finally, to Mad's. Madigan locked his gaze with mine as his lips closed around my finger to suck on the tip. I could see in him a warning for us to hurry. "Be safe," I cautioned.

"Aye. She can't run, so ye might have to carry her. Her leg's got a heavy limp if she uses it too much."

I nodded and scurried down the steps, noting Annabelle's slight limp that looked like a handicap she was well used to. Something told me she hadn't acquired it during the stampede yesterday. "Can I pick you up?"

Annabelle nodded, though she didn't look too sure of her answer. I was a total stranger to her, but I think the fact that I had the title of 'Princess' before my name gave me a little extra credibility. I hitched her bony body up on my hip, surprised and worried at how light she was.

Bastien's arm gravitated to the small of my back as he started us off at a brisk pace. He kept checking over his shoulder, making sure a wildebeest or whatever wasn't bearing down on us.

Apparently we should've been checking our right, which was where the... I don't know how to explain it, but skulking toward us with serpentine grace was none other than a... well, a porcupine monster the size of a full-grown bear. The brown beast had foot-long quills jutting out all over its body. I tried to reconcile the beast with the tiny porcupines I'd seen up in Common, grimacing at the janky razor-sharp teeth sticking out of its long, dragon-like face. From the neck down, it was a porcupine, but from the shoulders up, it was a dragon. I bit off a scream and bolted as fast as I could toward the castle that was unrealistically out of reach. Annabelle clung to me, crying in worried gulps as she clawed at my neck.

"Run to the castle and bolt the doors behind you!" Bastien pushed us ahead, leaving us so he could fight off the peluda like the badass he was. Armed with nothing but a dagger and his crazy fighting style that held nothing back, Bastien hurled himself at the massive thorny beast. The peluda had a long neck and a pointy dragon-like head, and seemed to hiss like a super pissed-off snake. The porcupine-dragon stalked toward us with a slither that held a dark intent.

Bastien had a dagger, and thankfully Montel, who came to his aid. I glanced over my shoulder as I ran, and saw Bastien punch the peluda square in the wet, leathery face, like they were in a bar and the peluda had hit on me or something. The vendetta seemed personal, though with Bastien, you never could tell. He swung wildly, but with precision enough to draw blood.

I ran with Annabelle, feeling like a tool for leaving the guys to fight the monster without me. Unarmed as I was, my job was to get the girl to safety. I didn't take my assignment lightly, but bolted through the village, not stopping to look at anything, but calling out a warning for everyone to get into their houses. "The peludas are here! Get inside and lock your doors!"

The trees whipped by us as I ran without slowing alongside the stream, Annabelle on my hip. A cry of relief broke from my lips when the palace came more fully into view.

"Papa!" Annabelle shrieked, stunning me temporarily with her sheer volume right next to my ear. "Help! Get Papa!"

I glanced to the focal point of her freakout and saw a peluda galloping toward us with a hungry gleam in his red eyes on the other side of the stream. He snorted and salivated, his claws pounding the dirt with determination. I took a chance and called out across the water, but didn't slow my sprint. "Stop! The *Voix* is telling you to go away," I ordered him, hoping my gift of talking to animals would work.

Bastien had been right; this wasn't simply an animal, or it would've been able to communicate with me. This was some sort of hybrid that didn't belong to the animal kingdom, and certainly didn't belong in Avalon. It was bent on destruction, and had its sights set on us.

The stream was about eight feet wide, and was the only thing separating us. I renewed my speed, hoping the monster's giant swinging belly made the distance too wide for him to leap across.

At some point, I'd like to think I would stop being surprised by the unpredictable things that happened in

Avalon, but when a loud fart exploded out the back end of the peluda and a quill was fired in my direction, I began to realize how underqualified I was to walk around in this country. I screamed and ran when the quill landed in my path and inexplicably caught on fire. I veered away from the stream, hoping a little distance would make the thick, steely quills less accurate with their aim.

Annabelle was sobbing when the peluda flopped its body into the stream, but I kept running, charging toward safety. I finally had the presence of mind to switch her to my other hip so I could press my ring to my heart and whisper a desperate, "Kerdik, Kerdik, Kerdik."

It was too much to hope he'd heard me, and way too much to count on him coming. If I'd been waiting on him when I was stuck in the well, I'd be a rotting corpse down there, for sure.

"He's underwater!" Annabelle cried, though this didn't sound like a victory, celebrating that the monster had drowned. "Hurry! The waves are coming!"

No sooner had she said this than the docile stream kicked up out of nowhere, turning a gentle lapping of two-inch waves into a multiplication of water. A rolling wave that was taller than me ripped through the stream from behind us, breaking and splashing too near for me to run unhampered. I tripped, but caught myself before face-planting.

I veered us further from the stream, astonished at the sheer mass of the waves piling high from such a modest water source. The peals crashed down, deafening us with their roar that was far louder than any beast.

I tried to keep my eyes on the castle, which was closer, but still way too far. I pumped my legs in desperation away from the stream until another porcupine-dragon monster came into view from the left. This one had light brown hair, but his quills were jet black and ready for battle. Angled back as they were, the quills looked like slick armor that moved with the wind. His dragon face snarled and hissed at us. As fast as I was, I knew we'd never make it in time.

"Link!" I screamed, hoping my voice would carry to the castle that was still a block away. I ran, though there wasn't much hope for my escape.

My heart swelled when the cavalry came. It wasn't Kerdik or Link, but a thick unkindness of ravens who swooped in and tried to peck out the peluda to my left's eyes. I let out a mournful cry when the peluda opened his mouth and let out a gust of gas that was sort of bluish in the direction of his miniature attackers. One by one, the ravens lost their flight, their balance, and I realized with dread, their lives. Their black feathery bodies crashed to the grass in motionless heaps, the chirp of *"Run, Princess!"* dying on their beaks.

I tried not to cry, but tears misted my eyes anyway at the sacrifice that was too great to quantify. A whole flock was giving their lives for my escape, and I was just friggin' letting them.

I was unarmed, and with a child. I wasn't sure what else I could've done in that moment, but I knew that years later, solutions would come to me, and haunt my nights.

Annabelle clung to me when we finally neared the steps of the castle. "We made it!" I cried.

Of course, I spoke too soon. A steely quill shot out from the peluda who was closing in from behind me. The tip of the quill was sharp as an arrow, and sunk into the meat of my calf, tripping me and landing me with a smack on the grass.

Then the arrow burst into flame, lighting my dress on fire.

21

TOO LATE

"Run, Annabelle! Go into the palace and get help!" I shouted, not sure how I had the presence of mind to even form coherent sentences.

The poor girl limped off as fast as she could, tears drooling down her face as she hobbled up the steps in search of someone to let her in, and save her from the monsters.

I jerked around and frantically smothered the fire that had caught on the hem of my dress. I needed to take one second and catch my breath, but I didn't want that satisfying inhale to be my last. Without bracing myself, I ripped the quill from my leg, howling as the blood poured out of me, soaking my shoe faster than I could scream about the pain. I tried to scramble to my feet, but my leg was being dramatic, and wouldn't let me walk. "Link!" I yelled, hoping someone would open the tall, forbidding doors for Annabelle, who was pounding with her tiny fist and calling for assistance. "Link! Help me!"

I could hear the peluda running toward me, hissing and huffing like a chubby guy jogging as he neared. I knew there was nothing I could do but brace myself for the fight I would surely lose. There was nothing to shield myself with, and nowhere to hide. I was so close to the palace steps, I could almost touch them, but the peluda wasn't about to let me crawl away.

Another quill shot into the same leg, just a few inches from where the last one sunk in. Volume like I'd never known erupted from me, reaching new heights and alerting the setting sun just how friggin' bad getting shot at point-blank range with a thick steel arrow hurt.

Again the fire burst out the end of the arrow, lighting the blackened edges of my gown up with orange flames, but it hardly mattered anymore. I was either going to die by burning alive, or by getting eaten by a magical porcupine-dragon. Bastien was nowhere near, though that was probably for the best. I didn't want him to know what it sounded like when the skin melted off my leg, or when my body was inevitably torn apart by a beast – make that two.

I looked up to face my killer, and saw two of them ambling toward me, their pace slowing, now that their prey was down for the count. I managed to smother the flames from what was left of my skirt, singeing my hands and thigh in the process. I coughed wildly, wishing for just one more kiss from Bastien, one more hug from my dad and Draper, and one more everything from Lane. I only hoped there was enough of my body left for her to bury when all was said and done. I ripped the second quill from my leg, my eyelids flaring open and then drooping at the rapid blood loss my body was struggling to keep up with. I'd donated so much blood to Avalon already, yet it seemed Faîte wasn't satisfied.

I gripped the quill to use as a weapon in my desperation, summoning with my crimson hand the courage to defend myself and Annabelle to whatever end was in store for us. My right hand pressed to my chest again, whispering the most fervent plea for my green BFF to come through for me.

My heart nearly leapt out of my chest when the front door banged open, the wood sounding almost angry with the thud it made to startle me and my attackers. I looked up, my vision blurring, my chest heaving, and saw him – Superman in all of his glory, wielding a kingly sword.

"Link, get my daughter into the house!" My dad bellowed, eyes fixed on the monsters who were circling their dinner.

I tried not to whimper, but the pathetic bleat couldn't be helped. The porcupine-dragons were closer to me than my dad was, and though he stalked toward us with measured steps, all they had to do was lunge, and I was a goner.

Link had his dagger in one hand and a full-on axe in the other. He followed close behind my dad after he shooed Annabelle into the safety of the palace. "Stay still, Rosie," Link instructed loudly, calculating the situation with clarity I couldn't. "I'll get ye out, but ye can't make any sudden movements." Then, disregarding his own advice, he jerked back and shouted, "Sluagh!" I glanced up to where he was pointing and saw ravens gathering in the sky, flying in from the west and forming a tight circle overhead. I couldn't understand their noises; I could scarcely comprehend anything beyond the agonizing pain. "Urien, the ravens are circling overhead! He's come for either you or Rosie. Rosie, come to me!"

That simple command was too much for the peludas to leave me open to a rescue. With a blast from their butts, a gaseous fire exploded out in a crack of thunder, lighting a line in the grass that separated me from the men who would save my life. Flames collected and grew, doubling and then climbing higher still as they licked at the earth around me. There was a line between me and the palace, and another that kept me from crawling back in the direction I came. The two peludas moved to either end of the dual rows of flames, boxing me in and making a clean escape impossible.

Link and Urien let out impassioned noises of anger and distress. The careful steps they'd moved to get near me was for nothing now. Untouchable as Link was, and royal as my dad was, it was all for nothing. Anger pricked my eyes when it settled in my stomach like an indigestible brick that I would die mere feet from my father and my friend. "Go!" I shouted above the roar of the flames. "You don't want to see this! Get into the house so they don't get you next!"

"We're not leaving you!" My dad bellowed, though I could hear the frustration in his voice. "We'll get you out, sweetheart."

The wind shifted and blew black smoke at me, filling my face with heat and my lungs with ash. I screamed when cinders leapt onto my dress and caught on what was left of the singed fabric of my skirt. I could feel the sting on my legs as I tried to suffocate the flames. I coughed like a smoker in search of just one last pure breath. The peludas started moving closer, their sinister sauntering was much too slow to be anything other than toying with me. Had they worn waxed mustaches, I'm sure they would have been twirling them by now while tying me to the train tracks.

I heard shouting and grunting outside the flames, and wondered if more peludas had joined the party. There were animalistic screams that gave me hope that the guys would escape somehow. I had no such optimism for myself, but spent the last of what I had on them.

I gave my only desperate hope one last shot of saving the day before I succumbed to the monsters who were intent that this would be my last minute. Pressing the ring to my heart and twisting the stones so they sank into my breast, I shouted, "Kerdik! Kerdik! Kerdik!"

I struggled to stand, but fell three times before I realized there would be no escaping. I collapsed back onto the grass and coughed, clutching the quill in hopes that I could fend off my enemy with its own weapon.

When the wind blew the other way, allowing me to see again as the ash and smoke wafted away from me, I shrieked at the sight of half a dozen snouts surrounding me on either ends of the two rows of flames. There was a whole village of people, but they were intent on getting me, as if I'd been the target all along. My heart sank at the perfectly orchestrated attack that I'd fallen for. Morgan would know that poisoning the wells would have only one cure, and with Lane gone, I was the clear choice for who would be out in the open, dressed for my royal role, and sitting on a throne with a target on my forehead.

Link fought with a peluda that had him and my dad trapped on the steps of the castle, waving his axe around and finally chopping off the peluda's head in the brawl. It was a victory, but it came too late. There were too many of them now, and I could see it dawning on my father as he fought with a second peluda who came up to take the fallen one's place, that these might be his last moments, as well.

I clutched the quill in my hand and whipped it around as best I could to fend them off, vowing that if I was to die tonight, I would go down swinging.

I heard a crack before the peluda on my right charged for me, clearing the distance in two wild gallops. The teeth that bit down on the leg that hadn't been shot with arrows were cruel, sinking into my skin and going straight for my ankle, crushing the bones without considering the fact that I totally didn't want him to do that. Agony ripped through me, but the monster wasn't satisfied with my howls. His clawed foot stomped down on the calf muscle I'd worked my whole life to maintain, shredding my skin to the bone like it was nothing.

Like, to the bone.

Like, I saw an inch of my shin bone.

The second monster shot me in the other thigh with one of its quills, bringing my screams to new heights.

Instead of ripping my leg off, the first peluda used his leverage on my shattered ankle to drag me away – to what end, I couldn't tell you. The searing white hot pain was everywhere, and I sorely wished he would just get it over with. The smoky air that hit my exposed shin bone felt like a torture I wished I could lose my mind to, but unconsciousness eluded me, letting me feel every jarring movement as I was dragged through the two rows of flames.

My adrenaline spiked, but coupled with my blood loss, it was too much for my body to handle. I went into some sort of shock, my nerves feeling every bit of torture while the fire died from my view. I saw only the night sky and the blue moon as my vision started to tunnel, making the world impossibly smaller, while the agony stayed so very big.

I don't know how I would've fended off the claw that came for my face, but as it ripped from my forehead down my cheek and across my chest, I wished for chainmail armor, or a flamethrower, or... something. Blood drooled and spurted out from my face and breasts, rendering me unrecognizable with half my face shredded so cruelly.

I heard a voice through my terror, taking me to a new level of get-me-the-crap-outta-here. It was that same gravelly, metallic voice belonged to the cloaked man who attacked me. Somehow he was here now, speaking to me from the opposite side of the flames, across the way from Urien and Link. "Madigan's new bride, at last. I told ye I would have your spirit," he reminded me. His voice was accompanied by the sound of birds' wings flapping, though I didn't see any feathered friends nearby – they were too smart to hang out here.

Link's voice, which was usually confident in all matters, quavered like a little boy's. "Get back! Ye can't have her."

"Mine now. So full of fight. All mine," the cloaked man chuckled darkly, and I heard him moving toward me.

The blue moon looked down on me in pity, wondering how I'd gotten into this mess to begin with. I blinked through my screams that somehow seemed separate from my body, sounding like they were coming from someone else. *That can't be me. I don't scream like that. Poor girl sounds terrified.*

The blue of the moon grew dim, and then mutated with a hue of green I couldn't make sense of.

I blinked my one good eye again, and Avalon, Common, and everything inside of me that had once burned so bright, all faded to black.

22

A STAR NAMED BRITNEY SPEARS

"Do you need to be reminded of what will happen to you if she doesn't wake up?"

Kerdik's voice roused me like a crack of a whip, sharp as it was.

Jean-Luc's reply sounded scared, but determined. *"Of course not. I know I signed away my life when I came to work for the king. Would you just back up? Hovering doesn't help me get the job done."*

"Her face! You've sewn her up to look like an old rag doll on one side. She was beautiful, but you've made her an eyesore."

"I'm doing the best I can! The peluda clawed clean through half her face! What healing powers do you imagine me capable of? I'm keeping her alive, which is a feat, let me tell you."

"And her legs still look terrible. She's an athlete in her world, so they need to be fully functional. There's no way she'll be able to walk ever again as she is now. I'll not have her confined to a chair for the rest of her days. I'd prefer her legs without burn marks and quill wounds all over them, too."

"Of course you would. You're always studying her in ways you shouldn't. She's a sweet girl, and doesn't need you staring at her legs."

Kerdik's voice turned sharper. "She's far too pale. Does she need more blood? Her father's donation clearly wasn't enough." I heard a rustle of material, and then a grave, "Use mine. I have far more magic than Urien. It'll heal her faster. Plus, it'll seal her against the Sluaghs coming to look for her again. They won't be able to steal her spirit if I seal it inside of her."

"But... I... To use your blood? That's a little over my head. There's so much mystery to you involved; there's no telling what it'll do to her. Where's my parchment? I have to tell him of the risks."

I drifted back to sleep, unable to fend off unconsciousness for too long. My world was a tornado of black and grey, swirling with pinpricks of stars the moment something sharp bit at my arm. The stars grew brighter, and somehow seemed loud, like I could not only see them, but hear their brilliance that sparkled in my ears. My senses felt like they were scrambling, tilting me and pushing something powerful through my lungs that I couldn't quite harness with any kind of certainty. The friction of the charge led to heat that threatened my cellular makeup on a level I couldn't compute. The surge left a trail of minia-ture explosions as it burned through my veins, changing atoms and altering things that were best left alone. I hadn't known this was what death would feel like. In truth, I assumed I was too stubborn to die, but perhaps that was my foolishness poking through.

I felt my throat scrape raw, and realized that my body must be screaming. I felt so removed from my skin that I couldn't connect the convulsing I knew my body was doing to my mind. The only thing I could hear was the sparkle of the stars, and boy, did they have a tune to rival the actual Britney Spears. They were so glorious that I couldn't focus on anything else – even the pain I was sure was there.

Then somehow *I was* the stars, teeming with them until they flew into my skin, like I was a magnet for the most brilliant of beauties. My body felt like it was glowing from the inside out, my cells heating and whirling with a force I was unfamiliar with.

A delicious heat started in my left eye, and then spread out through my face. It ran like a line of too-warm choco-late over each of the claw marks that had left me disfigured and barely alive. I knew my body was convulsing as my heart started to give up the fight, but as the light and heat spread through me, I didn't care. I was a star, twinkling and shining above the pain and the fear of the unknown. If my afterlife would be spent as a star, looking down at the world with a brilliance to light the way, I would take it.

The warmth moved over my chest and through it,

doing something to my lungs that gave them more air, like a balloon that inflated too quickly. The heat bowled through my veins, rolling down my arteries and filling them with that same melty chocolate. It all felt like a surreal dream I couldn't quite get ahold of. On and on it churned through my body, until it seemed every part of me was brimming with warmth and gooey deliciousness.

The agony of dying was finally passing, and now I was in limbo, resting from the torment Faîte had put me through.

The star that morphed with me twinkled, turning its brightness up to a decibel that finally grew too painful for me to stand. One last scream erupted from me, and then I knew nothing, felt nothing, and was blissfully nothing.

DEAD WITH KERDIK

The arms around me were comforting and warm. The scent of grass, daisies and roses greeted me, wrapping me in the closeness of a haven I thought I might never feel again. The muscles were firm, though not as broad and gratuitously beefy as Bastien's. I wondered where my boyfriend was, and if he was looking for me, or if he was still out slaying dragons.

My hand dragged up the fabric of Kerdik's pressed shirt, clumsily clutching at the nuances of his pectoral muscles to make sure he was real. "Darling? Rosie, are you awake? Did it work?"

My eyelids felt heavy with too many burdens when they finally opened. We were on a raised wooden bedframe, but there was thick, soft grass where the mattress should have been. My gaze widened, and I saw that we were on our nature bed in the middle of a meadow, surrounded by millions and millions of daisies and roses that boasted every color of the rainbow. The sun shone down on us, warming our skin, but not blinding me with its brilliance.

"Water?" I rasped, unsure where I was at in this new afterlife.

"Of course, love. Let me just move you up a little. There you go." He shifted against the wooden headboard of the bed that wasn't mine, and cupped his hand to my lips, angling it downward as water welled in his palm. The trickle into my throat felt amazing, cooling me and refreshing too many weary things to count.

I swallowed over and over until my stomach protested. "Oh, that was amazing. Thanks, K." I looked up at his face, which was gazing on me with a mixture of devotion and wariness. My body didn't feel sturdy enough to sit up on my own. I felt oddly boneless, so I stayed tucked in Kerdik's embrace, my cheek resting on his shoulder, his body soothing mine as his chest moved steadily up and down. I pursed my lips, afraid the peace of the moment was too unrealistic to trust. "Which parts of it all were real? Am I... Are we dead?"

"Do you feel dead?"

I looked down and saw that my legs were perfect – without even the scar from when Remy had sliced the snakes out of my thigh. My skin looked different, though. Instead of my usual tan, the flesh was lighter, with a peachy glow that seemed too creamy and reflective to be real. I nodded slowly. "I think this is dead. My skin's practically shining. That's not what my body looks like." I listened for any nearby voices, but couldn't make out so much as a bird. "I can't hear anyone. Usually I can pick out something, but it's just us. This is... Yeah, this is dead. I can't even hear any animals." I studied the flowers, fascinated that this was where I'd ended up. I'd never given much thought to the afterlife, but if this was it, I wasn't about to complain. "Wow. I must've done something good to end up here. So pretty."

Kerdik's free hand rested on my bare knee, drawing attention to the fact that I was wearing one of my cotton strappy nightgowns. This one was white, and added to the glow of my new afterlife peachy skin, increasing the Heavenly ambiance.

"Bastien's alive, then? And Dad and Link? They survived?"

"They did."

I looked around again, and the way my neck moved, it felt like my head was floating. Kerdik and I had died together – it was the only way to explain how we'd ended up here, alone in Heaven while the world was still in turmoil. "Did it hurt when you died? Mine was a lot of pain."

His eyebrows pushed together. "Are you in pain now?"

"No. I don't think so. I feel... is this what being high feels like? I don't totally know what's happening here."

"What would you like to have happen?"

I considered this, but soon my brain started to strain with answers that were stacked on top of more questions. "Too many things," I replied simply. My lashes fluttered shut as I gave up on figuring the afterlife out just yet. I leaned back into Kerdik's shoulder, snuggling up to his long body and pulling my knees up so I could be as close as possible.

His fingers trailed from my knee down the slope of my unmarked calf and swirled on my big toe, giving it a playful little tug. "Can you feel that?"

"Mm-hm," I answered dreamily. "Feels like you love me."

I could hear the smile in his reply. "Indeed, I do. I never thought I would do for anyone what I did to try and save you. I didn't realize how much I truly loved you until I thought I might lose you forever."

"Whatever you did to try and save me must be what killed you. Kerdik, I'm so sorry." The words sounded trite, but I couldn't think in a straight line with all this newness swirling in my brain.

"Don't think on it," he whispered like a promise that everything would be alright.

I tried not to dwell on all the awful ramifications of being dead. "Do you think we'll have each other forever?"

"I think we already do. You should know better than to mark people so permanently. At this rate, I'll never be able to shake the affection I have for you." His fingers trailed back up my calf and drew a lazy circle on my knee. "I'm sorry it took me so long to come when you called."

I shrugged. "I'm dead now. What do I care? Let's just be here for a few before we crash into the mountains of regret. I can't process it right now. I'll be too sad about all the people I love that are left behind."

"Then what shall we talk about?"

My lips pursed and drew to the side in thought. "What are you most looking forward to, now that you can do anything without worrying about how it affects the world?"

Kerdik chuckled. "That you think I concern myself with the daily woes of Avalon shows how little you know me." He considered my question, and then spoke his confession quietly. "If I couldn't hurt anyone, I would strip you naked and make love to you. If there was no fear of you turning into a..." He cleared his throat. "I would pledge my body to yours over and over until mine was the only name in your heart." His thumb trailed over the outline of my face just to feel the texture of my impossibly smooth skin. It wasn't from Jean-Luc sewing me up, but whole new flesh that was velvety to the touch.

My eyes widened and my jaw dropped. "Wow. I wasn't expecting such an honest answer. I was thinking more along the lines of you wearing women's underwear while lighting off illegal fireworks or something."

"I much prefer the fire we make together."

I snuggled more firmly into him, pressing into the

wound he probably didn't want me to know was there. "Roland told me about Tara. You fell in love with her and had sex, but it turned her into a sea monster-dragon. Then she killed herself in the ocean. I'm so sorry."

Kerdik's eyes tightened. "Then you know of my curse?"

I nodded slowly, hoping he wouldn't snap at me.

"You know, and yet you're still in my arms."

My heart hammered in my chest when he traced his finger along my lower lip. Our eyes locked in on each other's, counting the irregular heartbeats that banged through my body. Something shifted, as it always did with us.

I was dead, and so was Kerdik.

He snuck his finger past my lips, gazing at me hungrily as my mouth closed around his finger. My tongue laved around his digit, sucking with just enough force to watch his eyes roll back. Bastien was alive, and I was very much dead. As much as I knew that would hit me hard all too soon, I was determined to enjoy the serenity of the moment. My fingers reached up and stroked along the edge of his angular jaw, feathering the green silky skin that always fascinated me.

When he lowered his lips to mine, my heart fluttered with all the fervency of a hummingbird's wings. Our other stolen kisses had either been accidents or fits of frustration, but this one was true and intentional. We both wanted this one. Perhaps we wanted too much for Faîte to be merciful, but it was our chance, so we took it.

24

ON OUR BED OF GRASS

The kiss started out slow and beautiful. Kerdik was careful with me, fingering the edge of my face as if I was made of glass. I didn't often feel graceful, but his feather-light touch made my body stretch like a ballerina's. My neck elongated so he could trickle his touch down my throat. My back arched when his arm coiled more firmly around my waist. I felt precious in his arms, and sucked on his lower lip when he made to pull away. I didn't want the kiss to end just yet. After dying by being ripped apart by a hoard of peludas, I wanted to feel like a dancer. My skin was glowing without a single scar to remind me that life had ended so unkindly.

My hand buried itself in the hair at the back of his head. My fingers tangled in the soft, short blue, frustrating the zig-zag part down the side. I gave a slight tug that made him deepen the kiss, his tongue sneaking past my lips to mingle with mine. My hand drifted of its own accord to the collar of his white pressed shirt, fiddling idly with the top button until it popped open for me.

Kerdik pulled back, his eyes wide as he took in my daring that was tinged with a brush of bashfulness. "I... You want..."

I shrugged. "I'm dead. What's the point of self-control? This is the first time I've felt beautiful in too long."

He inhaled at my logic, and then leaned in to kiss me again, leaving me breathless before he pulled away. He sat us both up straight, and turned my body around so my back was pressed to his chest, explaining with a reminder of, "The fire. I don't want my only shirt singed."

"Oh, right. That's still coming." I waited for the belch to build in my esophagus, but after half a minute of patience, it never came. "Huh. I mean, I don't feel like I need to breathe fire. Maybe being dead got rid of that little tick." I stood up and hopped off the bed. It was a glorious feeling to stretch my arms over my head, digging my toes in the grass. I leaned down to pick a daisy from the green, and set to work braiding the stem into my hair. Braiding my hair and picking flowers would be my new job.

Kerdik watched me with concern, but I couldn't have felt more like a hippie love child if I tried. I was wearing a pure white nightgown that kind of looked like a sundress, standing in a field of flowers with a nature bed smack in the middle of the perfect scene. If this was dead, I'd be sad about it tomorrow. The sun was too deliciously warm for complaining. There were no peludas here. After having my face nearly clawed off, dead didn't feel too bad a place if I could see out of both eyes, and could walk without issue.

"I don't understand," Kerdik admitted, his eyebrows pushed together. "You should be breathing fire by now."

I braided a second flower into my curls, that I could tell had been washed recently. "Sorry to disappoint. Maybe you should kiss me again. And again, and again, and again." I smiled at him and waved for my friend to join me. "We're dead, K. I don't think this world has the same rules or consequences. If I'm my biggest adventure, then this is what I want to do at the finish line of it all."

Kerdik rose slowly, his eyes suddenly hungry as he took in my form. He cleared the gap between us in two long steps, laying one on me as he cupped my face. My knees went weak with the passion that didn't bother with politeness. Our lips made a perfect mess of our friendship, and then our tongues followed the bad example. After trying to please my parents, Bastien, and Avalon, doing the wrong thing tasted like peppermints and sheer deliciousness.

Kerdik had always been the treat I wasn't allowed to savor.

"Closer," he panted. "I need more." He clutched my hips, so I went with the moment and jumped up into his arms, wrapping my legs around his waist. I sucked his grunt of surprise and longing into my mouth, taking his gasp and making it my own. His left hand wandered into no man's land, giving my round rear a luscious squeeze. "More," he breathed.

He carried me to the bed and dumped me there, grabbing hold of my foot so he could rub sweetness into the sole while I stretched on the green of the grass mattress. I moaned pornographically at the steady pressure of the massage, my body going from live wire to limp in a matter of seconds. Kerdik's mouth was in a tight line, and I could practically feel the lust radiating off him when my nightgown slipped up my leg a few inches.

I'd been the ugly girl my whole life. I mean, no man in Common had looked at me as if I was beautiful, much less sexy. The heated look in Kerdik's eyes was the way every girl wishes she could make a man lust for her. The ugly girl who was still inside of me high-fived the vixen in bed, and told her to make the most of the opportunity she'd never had.

Then suddenly, Kerdik dropped my foot and backed away, his wide eyes wary with caution, looking at me like I was a danger to him. "You'll not tempt me further with things we simply cannot do."

"Hello, you're the one who kissed me like Ian Somerhalder on a mission, and then grabbed my butt." I sat up and studied his expression, trying my best to put my libido on hold. "What's wrong, K? If I'm not breathing fire, then who's to say we can't enjoy this?"

His expression closed off, but then dipped back into the land of lust. "I don't know, Rosie."

I sat up, frowning. "Well, if you don't know, that's alright, but you probably shouldn't kiss me like that until you do."

"Yes, well, perhaps I'm tempting myself with forbidden fruit." He took tentative steps toward the mattress, leaning over and kissing me lightly, but with a dark intent that made my blood race. Kerdik tipped me back onto the green, grassy bed and climbed up my body, resting his hands on either side of my head. He parted my knees and pressed his hips down onto mine, taking our weird friendship past the hazy boundary and planting it square where it might never return from. His whisper in my ear made my body react against his, writhing when I should've stayed still. "I know exactly what to do with a ripe piece of fruit." He kissed my chin, then my throat, then my collarbone as I fisted the grass, tearing it out by the roots. "So sweet. It would be delicious if we fell." He slid the strap off my shoulder with one of his dexterous hands, studying my body that, in death, had absolutely no self-control.

One quick tug, and our friendship would take a back burner to the passion that blazed just beneath the surface. He left me in limbo to squirm while he moved over my torso, nipping at me through the fabric in all the right, and oh-so-wrong places.

"I could tease you like this for an eternity," he said as he gripped my thighs.

Something in his words pinged reality into my hazy

brain. "Wait, you're immortal. I get how I'm dead, but how are you dead?"

Kerdik's face lifted from his conquest, quirking an eyebrow at me. "That's what you're thinking about? I've got you inches away from naked, and that's where your mind is at? Perhaps I am rusty."

I shook my head, embarrassed. "No! Nothing like that. I'm totally all over the place. I suck at being dead. I'm sorry." I cupped his cheeks and brought him up so his face was hovering over mine. "I don't understand. How did you die?" I gave his lips a light peck. "Talk to me."

"You were bleeding out, so I told Jean-Luc to infuse you with some of my blood. I thought it would bring you back, but you died, and then the sacrifice killed me, as well." He brushed his nose across mine and reached down to pinch my thigh just to watch me squirm beneath him. "We don't need to talk about such things now. You were right; let's make the most of this place."

I gasped, but it wasn't because of his confession. His skin that I loved started to change, the green swirling with a dark, muddy crimson. It looked like when you first drip a dribble of food coloring dye into liquid, but don't mix it all the way in. The cloudy feathery color fanned out across his face, but didn't permeate completely. "Kerdik, what's happening?" I inched out from under him and scrambled off the bed, horrified at the change. "What is that?"

"What?" He looked down as he rose to his knees on the bed, perplexed when he didn't see anything unusual.

I pointed, confused and afraid. "Your skin! It's doing something freaky! Why is it red?"

Kerdik scowled, affronted that I would kick him where it hurts. "My skin is green, as you very well know. You yourself once told me it was beautiful. Was that a lie to manipulate me?"

I shook my head in rapid jerks. "No! The green's gorgeous, and you know it. But it's red now! Your skin's got red swirling through it. How can you not see that?" I backed away when he moved off the bed and stepped toward me, still examining his skin.

"What are you talking about? There's no red anywhere."

"Right there! Right where I'm pointing is a huge patch of it!" I took a cautious step forward and touched the spot on his cheek as it started to shrink, fading away so he could be his normal self again. "Well, what happened to it? It was just here. It was all over you, this dusty pinkish-reddish color swirling all over your skin. It looked like a gas or something, but like, part of your skin."

He looked at me as if I'd lost my mind. "Rosie, I'm telling you, nothing like that just happened to me. I've never even heard of something like that in Avalon."

"I know what I saw! Your skin was... but then it wasn't!"

Kerdik placed his hands on my shoulders to look deep into my eyes. He studied my worry for a few beats, and then put on a kinder expression. "You're troubled. You've been through a lot. Let's calm things down for a bit. You're seeing things. No matter what world you're in, that can't be good."

I gulped, worried that I might spend my second life with nine shades of crazy dancing around in my brain. "It was so real. You promise me you didn't see anything?"

"I promise. Let's calm things down for a minute."

"My skin is different," I blurted out, worry creeping up on me and taking hold of my mind. I was unable to live in bliss anymore, and wanted serious answers. "Why is my skin lighter and peachy? Is that what happens when people die?"

"How should I know? This is just one of the changes your body's experiencing, now that you're dead."

"It's doing it again!" I pointed at his face, jumping back in fear. "Your skin's changing colors! It's that pinkish-red again! It's swirling all over you. You really can't see it?"

"Could you not point and shriek at me like a peasant? You're the one person who's never done that to me. You know how that hurts me."

I held up my hands. "I'm sorry. You're totally right. You know I love your green skin. I wouldn't change a thing about it. It's not the green that's freaking me out, it's the reddish color that doesn't belong."

"Your mind is playing tricks on you. Let me think for a second. What's the trigger?"

"I don't know. Both times, we were just talking."

Suddenly, Kerdik froze with his shoulders tensed, but gave no indication that he could see the shift. When he finally spoke, his voice came out cautious. "Wait until it goes away, and then ask me a question. Anything you already know the answer to."

"Huh?"

"Just humor me. Is it gone yet?"

I watched the colors dance on his skin before they faded, as if a breeze blew the cloudiness away. "It's gone." Despite my growing anxiety, I threw my arms around Kerdik's neck. "I'm sorry I pointed like that. It was so mean. I wasn't thinking." I kissed his lips, savoring it when he lingered. "You know you're devastatingly handsome, right?"

A small smile played on the edges of his mouth. "I believe you've mostly called me beautiful, but never handsome. I rather like the sound of it." A low noise of contentment resonated in his chest. "You have no idea what that does to a man."

I kissed him again, standing on my toes to compensate for his superior height. "I love you. You know that, right?"

He looked deep into my eyes, as if he was really, truly seeing me as I was. Despite my new skin, he saw the me I'd brought from one life to the next, which reminded me that I was still in there. His knuckles brushed across my cheek, and he kissed me again. "I do. And I think it's plain to everyone who's ever seen us together that you ran off with my heart from the very first moment we met." Our lips didn't like being apart, so we kissed again, and a few more times after that. Finally Kerdik took a step back, which was the only way we might stop kissing each other. He held my hands and swung them between us, being downright adorable and freaking irresistible. "Is the red gone now?"

"Yes. You wanted me to ask you a question I know the answer to?"

"Please."

"Okay, then what's your name?"

He smirked at me and answered truthfully. "My name is Kerdik." He swung our hands between us lightly, as if we were kids in a meadow with no cares at all. "Is my skin still green? Any trace of the red?"

I undid his cuffs and folded them up so I could see his forearms. I don't know what it was about a man's forearms that drew me in, but Kerdik had an elegance to his musculature that I liked gawking at. "Not a spot."

"Ask me again."

"Your name? Okay. What's your name, guy-I'm-just-meeting?"

He replied with a succinct, "My name is Dub."

My eyebrow quirked at the odd choice for a lie. I dropped contact as the dusky rose color swirled up in him again. I didn't mean to hop backwards, but the distance between us seemed necessary. "Why is it doing that?"

Kerdik nodded once, having all the information he needed. "Because I lied to you. Obviously my name's not Dub. You're seeing my lies."

25

KISSING ON A GRASSY BED OF LIES

My eyes widened and my mouth fell open. "Are you serious? How am I seeing lies? Wait, what did you lie about the other times?"

Kerdik's shoulders deflated. He reached out and pulled me closer, wrapping my arms behind him and looping his around me so that we were stomach to stomach. His shirt and vest were still buttoned, but freshly ravished by yours truly. He was dapper and manly, and now that I was allowed to see him in this new afterlife with no other responsibilities or ties, I could fully appreciate just how much he made my heart flutter. He kissed my lips again, inhaling the fragrance of my skin as if he was afraid it would be the last time. "Just in case you're too angry with me to do that again."

My voice came out wary. "What did you do?"

"You're quite certain you don't want to try making love first? I conjured this entire field to captivate you."

My eyebrows furrowed. "You didn't make the field. This is just where we landed when we died." I glanced around at the flowers, wondering if there was a number to the millions of petals that seemed to burst with equal measures of serenity and sunshine.

"I love you, Rosie. No matter what, hold that tight in your heart as a truth that won't change."

I cast up a baleful look. "Hello, your moods change on a dime. I'll take the love while you're handing it out, though. I like you in love. You smile more. You're not Kerdik the Terrible, or whoever you think you need to be to keep people on their toes."

"But darling, don't you know?" He brushed his nose to mine with a sweetness that made my toes curl. "I am terrible."

"Not here, you're not. You're just mine, and I love you like that."

He kissed me again, still with that cautious inhale that told me he knew I would bolt. "Then yours I shall be." My body molded itself to his easily, as if we'd been holding ourselves back from a dance we already knew the ending to.

"What did you lie about?"

Another indulgence between us passed before I released his lower lip from my teeth. Kerdik cleared his throat and grabbed onto my left hand, holding it out to the side, while keeping my hips secured to his with his other arm. He started to sway side to side with me, summoning up the right words while we danced to the soundless music of our meadow. Of all my life experiences, I would never stop loving it when Kerdik danced with me.

"The peludas tore you up before I got to you. I should've come sooner. When I disappear, it's not because I want to leave you. It's usually because I'm searching for..." He shook his head. "But that's a story for another time. I was preoccupied, but on your third call I felt the urgency. I found you, but it was already too late. Your femoral artery was torn open, and you'd already lost too much blood. And your face..." He didn't finish his sentence, but shuddered at the memory. "Your eye was cut, and half your face was a mangled, bloody mess."

The story and our dance had to pause so he could kiss me again. We were both grateful that I could see out of both eyes, and that my face still looked like me.

"I've caught glimpses of your breasts on marvelous occasion, but seeing them mangled how they were? I couldn't bear it. Your body is..." He cleared his throat and went back to our dance. "If *I* couldn't have your body, I at least wanted you to be able to give it to whom you wished, whole and beautiful."

"I'm sure Bastien would've appreciated the thought." His name tasted wrong on my tongue. I didn't want to think about Bastien if I couldn't have him. Just like when he'd left, saying his name was painful.

Kerdik's face soured. "Bastien's ungrateful. He doesn't realize the rarity you are. He's Untouchable, so he's used to women throwing themselves at him. Let him walk around with green skin that people shriek at, and see how much he appreciates every brush of your hand then."

I leaned up on my toes and kissed my Kerdik again. "Shush about that. I don't want to talk about the life I can't have. I'm serious. When I had to leave Judah, I tried not to talk about him. Too painful. I don't want to talk about Bastien now. I can't think about never seeing him again. I can't go there, or I'll never stop crying."

Kerdik cleared his throat and straightened his posture, leading the dance with elegance and unhurried familiarity. My feet fell in line, though I'd never done this dance before. "Very well. The point is, I couldn't bear it, and you were bleeding out. Jean-Luc gave you a blood and magic transfusion from your father, but it wasn't enough. Jean-Luc was able to keep you from death for a time, but your heart kept slowing to almost a stop, no matter what we did. It was terrifying." He closed his eyes. "I haven't known fear like that in a long time."

"Oh, sweetie." I reached up and kissed him again, which seemed to center us both. Now that we could kiss without me breathing fire or having a boyfriend, it seemed we couldn't get enough, but kept going back in for another taste, and another. In a word, Kerdik was delicious.

He kissed me three more times before he continued. "You were unrecognizable, and most likely would have walked with a limp, if you managed to walk again at all. I couldn't stomach the thought of you hobbling through life, losing half your vision, and showcasing too many scars. I didn't know what else to do." He looked down with a tinge of guilt. "You're the only one who gazes at me like you do. It's powerful, and makes me feel like I can do things I'd long put out of my mind. That person I disappeared to go search for? It's a quest I didn't think myself worthy of until you looked at me with those adoring eyes that made me feel unstoppable."

"Hello, you actually are unstoppable. That's got nothing to do with how I look at you; it's pure fact."

"Being it and believing it are two different things. Plus, the things that stop immortals are on a different level than mere mortals. I have my own unique limitations, but I needed you to come along and rekindle the fire I'd long given up on." He leaned in for another kiss, addicted as I was to the flavor of us. "I needed you to look at me like that, and with both eyes. Your sliced one wasn't responding to light. It had this dead, glazed look to it I couldn't bear."

"Aw, man! That totally sucks. I don't have a mirror here. Do they look normal now?"

"Of course they do," he said dismissively.

I gasped and shook my head when the swirls of red took over again. "You're lying! I can see it all over your face. What's wrong with my eyes?" I patted my lashes, horrified that I might be walking around with one ginormous troll eyeball shoved into my ocular cavity or something.

Kerdik looked up at the sky and muttered a frustrated curse under his breath. "Well, I suppose I can't lie to you, can I? They're vibrant and focused, and that adoring look I need to survive is still there. But the eye that was cut," he said, reaching between us to thumb at my cheekbone below my left eye, "it's a different color now."

I jerked away, shocked that something had changed so drastically. "What? How could you not have said something sooner? What color are my eyes now?"

Kerdik held onto my forearms to steady me. "Your right eye is still blue, but your left one is peach now."

My mouth fell open. "What?! Did death give me albino traits or something? What the crap, K? How did a cut change my eye color?"

He swallowed, looking guilty and a little afraid of my reaction. "I had Jean-Luc infuse your veins with some of my blood. I've only heard of an immortal doing this for a mortal once before. It was a wild guess, but it worked! You look like you again, more or less."

My nose scrunched, vaguely recalling Kerdik's command to Jean-Luc, to infuse me with his blood while I was in and out of consciousness. I looked up at Kerdik with astonished admiration. "That's the second time. You told Bellamy to infuse the tattoo ink with your blood."

"Yes, but that didn't go into your veins. It was a drop or two for your tattoo, so I could locate you more easily, should you need me. This was more. This was a lot of blood and a lot of magic that went out of me and into you."

"But you don't like to share your magic."

"I guess that rule doesn't apply to you, among the many others you tend to disregard." His slight tease did nothing to quell the love that swelled in me for the man who'd broken his own rules to try and save my life.

"I'm sorry it didn't work. That's epic love, Kerdik. Truly. Thank you for trying. I know you like to keep your magic to yourself." I lowered my chin, emotion rising in my chest. "Giving me your magic killed you. I killed someone I love." My hand flew to my mouth, wishing I could make those words untrue somehow. Tears wanted to birth from my eyes, but I shoved them down deep. I knew once I got started on all my regrets, I might never be able to stop. My words came out choked, blasting from me in a flurry of self-loathing. "Kerdik, I killed you! My love killed some-body again? My love killed you!" My knees started to shake, so I lowered myself to the edge of the grassy bed before they gave out. I wrapped myself in a hug I didn't deserve. I was a terrible person, to wield love that was so lethal. "My love killed Demi!" I confessed, my heart tearing anew. "My love killed Demi, and now it's killed you! I'm a horrible person! I'm so sorry, Kerdik. I didn't know! How can you still want me after I did something so awful?"

Kerdik rubbed his forehead in consternation, looking as if he wanted to say something, but was uncertain where to start. "Rosie, it's not what you think. Let me explain." He cast around for the right words, but when his gaze locked in on my eyes, he seemed to find himself once again. "I don't regret giving you my blood. I don't regret anything about you, so I don't want you to waste your time crying over the lost souls you couldn't save. Your love saves me every time I think I'm lost for good. You're always their princess; but you're always my queen."

"I love you so much," I admitted. "The friend part of us is my favorite thing some days."

The corners of Kerdik's lips tipped up as he gazed down at me. "You're my favorite thing, as well." He pulled me up to stand in his embrace, and I realized with a sudden peace that I never wanted to leave.

I closed the breath of a gap between us and kissed him, fiddling with the buttons on his shirt until the second one from the top came loose. Maybe I was making bad decisions. I was dead, so I decided not to care about the long-term ramifications of my actions. "No more serious talk. You're wearing too many clothes." I sucked on his lower lip as I quickly undid the buttons on his gray vest. "You're always teasing me, looking so tucked and unwrinkled." It made me want to make a perfect mess of his controlled demeanor.

"*I* tease *you*? Darling, you have no idea."

My libido flared when his arms wrapped around my hips to grab what he wanted. We were pressed tightly together, locked in a kiss that had a rough and unpolished desire fanning the fire that raged in us both. My knees were weak, but the rest of me was bold and ready. I decided we shouldn't waste any more time with teasing.

I decided we shouldn't waste any more time at all.

I finished unbuttoning his vest and shirt, exciting us both by running my palms over the planes of his chiseled chest. "Make love to me, Kerdik."

26

THE BLOODY TRUTH

I wanted more, always more – especially in this land of no consequences. But when I reached down and popped the button on his chocolate-colored trousers, he flung himself backward, taking several steps away from me. "Stop! I lied to you, Rosie. This is all a lie." He motioned around the meadow, and then ran his hands over his face. "We're not dead. My blood saved you, but you were convulsing, and then your body started to glow. Then the walls started shaking, and I couldn't tell if the unstable power was coming from me or from you. I wasn't sure what would happen, so I grabbed you and vanished us here. I was worried one of us might bring down the house on Urien or something!"

I stumbled back, the shock washing over me. "You... But you said! And then I..." The blood drained from my face. "How could you let me do that to Bastien?! You just let me walk around here thinking I was dead this entire time? You're a jerk! That's low, even for you. Why? Why wouldn't you tell me that I was alive?"

Kerdik's shoulders lowered, but his agonized expression composed itself with an air of professionalism. He slowly buttoned up his pants, shirt and vest as he spoke. "Because I was seduced by the idea that we could be together. When you kissed me and didn't breathe fire? That was the first time that's happened to me in decades. So yes, I wanted to take it as far as you'd let it go. I wanted to be with a woman who I didn't have to worry would turn into a dragon, or who'd have to stop every few minutes to burp fire. I was just a man, and you were simply a woman, and this world was ours. That's why I didn't tell you right away."

"There aren't words," I seethed, feeling the layers of his betrayal cutting deep. "You should've set me straight the very second I thought I was dead." I grabbed my forehead, horrified at my behavior as images of what I'd almost done with Kerdik slammed into my brain. "Oh, I'm working my way toward getting back with Bastien! I'm a terrible person!" I closed my eyes, hugging myself around the middle. "I'm so embarrassed! I thought this was someplace without rules or something. I threw myself at you! Did I ask you to have sex with me while panting like a hooker?"

"I would never call you a hooker, no." He rolled his eyes. "Your pesky conscience is so inconvenient. You didn't cheat on Bastien. You two aren't even back together. You thought you were dead, and you'd never see him again. Would you have spread your legs for me if you knew you were alive?"

"No! And don't say it like that," I balked, mortified. It was all too much. "Oh, but I did! We haven't even been on an actual date before, and I begged you to have sex with me. Who does that?"

He stepped closer and wrapped his arms around me, looking down at my distress with the scolding smile of someone who knew better. "Darling, you're exactly who I've always loved, just uninhibited. And we didn't do anything we haven't both thought about a thousand times already. We could have had sex up here for ages until we were both finally sated, and you would've thanked me for the lie that set you free." His fingers feathered the shell of my ear. "Any man would tell you whatever lie it took to get between your thighs. I'm an immortal, sure, but I'm also a man."

I gasped, and then did something I didn't think either of us would forgive me for. I pulled my hand back and let it fly, slapping him clear across the face. "Don't talk to me like that!"

Kerdik froze, his hand on his cheek to verify that the sting of my smack was indeed real.

My eyes widened as I took several steps back. "I'm sorry, Kerdik. I shouldn't have..." I smoothed my hands down the front of my nightgown over and over, afraid of myself for being such a whorish monster. I looked left and then right, realizing that the Heaven I'd thought we were in was actually a world away from where I wanted to be. Moisture pricked my eyes, and I knew I didn't want to break down in front of him. "I, um... I'm all messed up right now. Which way gets me out of here?"

Kerdik didn't answer me, but stared, still stunned that I was capable of hurting him. When a tear trickled down my cheek, Kerdik stumbled backward, as if *I* was something to be afraid of.

I turned around, wanting to ditch more than anything. "This way looks good," I said as I started off at a brisk pace. More tears gathered, and my vision started to cloud with an odd crimson blur. I was grateful no one saw the cascade of tears that joined that first solitary admission that Avalon, Common, and even fake Heaven were capable of making me forget who I was.

"Rosie, wait! Your eyes!"

I swiped at my tears, but jerked back when something red caught the edges of my vision. I looked down at the back of my hand and saw that it was smeared with a streak of blood where there should've been tears. "Oh! I think I'm bleeding."

Kerdik ran ahead and cut me off, blocking my path toward, let's face it, friggin' nowhere. "Rosie, oh! Stop crying!" he commanded, scrambling to wipe away my tears with his sleeve. He hated getting his shirts dirty, but he sacrificed his borderline OCD for me, caring for me after

I'd slapped him. He stood before me and leaned down to dab at my cheeks.

There's something poetic and perfectly precious about a friend who wipes your tears away. It's miraculous that a person can love you through your fractured and vulnerable moments; yet even more incredible is that you can learn to let someone be good to you. I trusted Kerdik with my shame, and he was gentle to me when I needed tenderness – liar though he was.

Of course, this kindness only made me weep more. "Don't be nice to me!"

"Darling, it's your tears! You have to stop crying. You're not cut anywhere that I can tell. Do you feel a cut on you?"

"No," I sniveled. "I don't want you to see me crying and gross. You hurt me, K! You took something beautiful and turned it into a filthy lie. I almost... I was going to... And now it's a joke! I'm a joke, and you did that to us."

"That's neither here nor there right now, my love. Your tears. They're not coming out like water. This blood is coming from your tear ducts! You're crying blood!"

I stumbled like I'd been struck blind, though I could see every daisy and rose petal perfectly. In fact, as my gaze flitted around the meadow, I realized it seemed I could see farther than I'd normally be able to. I hadn't paid that oddity much notice before, but chalked it up to the weirdness of the afterlife. I touched my eyes, letting out a horror movie-like shriek of terror when my fingers came away coated in blood. "What's happening to me? Make it stop!"

"I can't make you stop crying. Take a breath. We'll figure this out, alright? Does it hurt?"

"No, but... but... blood! This is blood! I'm crying blood!"

Kerdik raised his hands with all the peace of mind of one who could calm a jumper. "Yes, you are. This is just a new development, is all. I've never given my blood to anyone before. It was bound to have some unexpected side effects."

"Side effects?" My breath started coming out in shallow pants, and I felt the beginnings of a full-blown panic attack. "Bleeding eyeballs isn't a side effect, it's a horror movie! I... I'm... I have to get out of here!" I didn't care where I was going, but I was determined to get there at a run. I whipped past Kerdik, pumping my arms as more blood dripped down my face, freaking me out beyond what simple logic could counteract.

I ran as fast and as far as I could, not caring that Kerdik was behind me, gaining on my speed with his own frantic pace. "Rosie, stop!" When we finally collided, it was because I couldn't see where I was going anymore. The blood droplets were thicker than normal tears, and clouded my reddening vision faster than the clear kind could. Kerdik caught me and steadied me in his arms as I batted at the air, trying to see, and also trying to get far, far away. "Darling, you have to calm down so I can help you."

"I'm a freak show! Who cries blood? I can't even see!" I tried to stumble on my path to nowhere, but Kerdik's arms wrapped around my middle from behind. He crushed my back to his chest, keeping me close enough that I couldn't swat at him.

I struggled with all my confused and unfocused might, until finally Kerdik dropped to his knees, taking me with him. He held me tight while I alternated between sobbing and screaming, his body encompassing mine everywhere he could. "I know it's frightening now, but we'll figure this out, okay?"

The red thickened again at his devotion to me, reigniting the panic I couldn't divorce myself from. "I can't see! I can't see! Help me!"

Kerdik wiped his hand over my face, washing it with water that actually did clear away enough of the emotion so that I could see. "There we go. Is that better?"

"It'll never be better! I don't belong here! I'm from earth. I used to be normal. I don't cry blood! I can't... I can't do this!" My breath came out in a wheeze, frightening my resolve and breaking me down so that I was a limp puddle of limbs in Kerdik's scrambling arms.

Kerdik turned me and wrapped my arms around his neck. Then he rocked back to sit on his butt and folded my floppy legs around his waist. I sobbed uncontrollably into his shoulder, my arms clinging tight to him, refusing to let go. He didn't say anything about me ruining his shirt, and I couldn't decide if that was an indicator that he was truly freaked out, or if it was because he loved me. "This is a small price to pay for your life," he reminded me. "So I spend my time making sure you have a blissful existence with no reason to ever shed a tear. Is that the worst thing in the world?"

I let out a laugh that was mixed with a sob into his shirt, unable to find the words to answer him.

Kerdik chuckled, though I'm not sure how he found the strength to seek out sunshine when my world felt so undeniably black. "I'll take that as you accepting my apology for letting you think you were dead."

I scoffed through my tears that just kept on coming. My emotion soaked his shirt, making him look like he'd been shot in the shoulder.

He kissed my cheek. "And I'll take that scoff as you telling me how very much you love me, and that if things were different, we could be together."

I tried to see the daisies and roses he'd summoned just to make my day, but the lovely world was tainted with a thick film of crimson again. I writhed against him, clawing at his shirt as the panic seized me again, consequently making the tears fall afresh. "I can't see! I can't see! Make it stop!"

Kerdik had the presence of mind to speak softly to me while I freaked out. "I can't very well make it stop if you're committed to crying." He washed my face until all traces of the red were gone. The front of both our white garments were soaked with red and pink streaks, looking like we'd both been recently murdered. His arms coiled around me, holding me closer so that my breasts were pressed to him, and he could whisper into my ear. "You're going to have to stop crying. I know you're upset that we have to leave this place. I know you're devastated that I didn't peel this little tease of a dress off you and lick every inch of your body." He caught my earlobe between his teeth and gave it a little tug. "Tell me how badly you wanted me to take you. I need to hear it."

My breath caught in my throat as I gulped at the lure his words had on me. Goosebumps broke out all over my skin. "We can't talk like that."

His lips tickled the shell of my ear, and though there was no one to hear us, he still kept his seduction to a whisper. "You shouldn't be sad that we'll go back to being friends who want to indulge in ways we shouldn't." He sucked on my other earlobe, and my breath started coming out in husky rasps. "You shouldn't want me, Rosie." His lips moved to my neck and sucked the skin there harder than I could resist. My eyes rolled back as my chest heaved. His fingers traced down my throat and slid the strap from my shoulder, exposing more of my cleavage and my vulnerability than either of us could handle. "Tell me to stop, Rosie," he murmured as the other strap fell. His hands moved beneath me to grab the swell he couldn't resist, squeezing my backside with the same desire I could feel pulsing through my veins.

The only sound I made was an unintelligible, guttural groan that only fueled us to make worse decisions. It wasn't a misunderstanding this time. I knew I was alive, and that a life with Bastien was still in the cards for me, only I was choosing to indulge in things I had no business doing, and with a person who wasn't known for being gentle.

When we kissed, the guilt worked like an aphrodisiac, urging me over the edge as my trembling fingers ripped Kerdik's vest and shirt open, not bothering with the troublesome buttons. I wanted to feel everything, to make him tremble as he coaxed me to melt. Our tongues battled, as they always did, but it wasn't until a low growl built in Kerdik's throat as he tipped me back to lie in the grass beneath him that I finally came to my senses. "No! This isn't... We can't be... I can't want this, and neither can you!"

Kerdik deflated slowly atop me, slowing our passion to mere cheek kisses that were silent apologies for what we almost did, and had no business doing. "I'm not sorry." He finally pulled his head back enough so that he could look at me. Seeing my tears, he rested on one elbow so he could wash my face once more. The kiss that found my lips was a simple pledge that we wouldn't be so reckless with something so precious again. We needed our friendship, and took a moment to pay reparation to what we'd almost lost in the heat of the moment. "I'll behave myself from now on." He kissed me lightly again. "I love you, and we'll figure everything out."

I nodded, rolling onto my side so I could bury my face in his bare chest, savoring the warmth of a man whom everyone else assumed was so very cold. Kerdik was always warm to me. "I love you, too." I tapped my chest to indicate the hole I felt that could no longer be ignored. "I can't want this."

He wound a damp curl behind my ear and ran his hand down my spine to soothe me. His eyes said so many things his mouth wouldn't admit to. "Do you want me to take you home now?"

I shook my head, burrowing into him and clinging to the shirt I'd ripped open. His naked chest was warm and comforting, and served to center me while my emotions tumbled around in my heart without a helmet. "Not yet. Could you just hold me for a while until it all goes away?"

"Darling," Kerdik cooed, tipping my chin up so he could brush his lips to mine once more. "I could hold you forever. Always their princess; always my queen."

27

KERDIK'S PRINCESS, BASTIEN'S CHARGE

When the interior of the palace materialized before my eyes, I wasn't expecting the screams that greeted me. Aimee looked like she wanted to throw her arms around me, but restrained herself to a mere shriek, stumbling backwards when she factored in that I was standing in Kerdik's arms. "The princess! The Avalon Rose is alive and returned to us!" She bolted to the front door, her skirt flying out behind her. "Montel, go send out riders to bring everyone home. The princess is back!"

We were in the foyer of Lane's palace, but Kerdik didn't like me so exposed, so he led me further inside. The servants flooded into the house like ants running from a fire, stopping short with mirrored noises of shock when I confirmed that I was alive and well.

"But you're covered in blood! Where are you cut? We

thought you dead, Princess!" Mercy exclaimed, her hand on her heart.

Her sister, Faith, gaped at me, "So much blood! Get the princess the healer!" They both took in the scope of Kerdik's stunning chest and looked away with expressions of dread.

"I promise, I'm all healed. This is old blood." I didn't move from Kerdik's embrace – the shrieks and pointing put me on edge. I clung to his torn shirt and burrowed into his chest while the servants started shouting out questions and thanking the stars that I'd been brought back safely to the kingdom. "Jeez, how long was I gone?"

Hope clutched her ample bosom. "Two days, your grace. Two days without a lady to lead the nation! Two days we thought you dead!"

They pointed at my skin, marveling at the color that indeed, still seemed to glow. Not like, glow in the dark, but it had a sort of ethereal luminescence to it that made you look twice (and point, apparently). Couple that with my damp and blood-streaked nightgown, and everyone was freaking out. I shrank into Kerdik's side, wishing that I wasn't being gawked at in my nightgown.

Kerdik's hand moved slowly up and down my spine, posturing as he protected my body with his embrace. "Is there not a healer in the household for my princess? Someone fetch me Jean-Luc." I didn't much care for his dictatorial tone, but I was too turned around to correct him. He lowered his voice, his tone softening only for me.

"It's alright, darling. They're just surprised to see you alive. You were far more on the edge of death the last time they saw you." He was soaked in my blood, too, but no one dared to question his appearance. No one even seemed to care about his wellbeing. My fingers tightened on his shirt to let him know that I cared, even though I knew the blood he wore proudly was all mine.

I managed a wan smile at the people who whispered and pointed at my skin, marveling at the color and the fact that I was healed and whole.

Kerdik turned sharp again. "Have you all forgotten who it is you're whispering about? Since when did it become customary to point and gossip about the princess? Do I need to remind you all how to behave? I promise, you won't like it if I'm angered. She might not order your beheading, but I have no problem making an example of you if you forget how my princess is to be treated."

At once the entire staff fell to their knees, heads bowed so low, their foreheads touched the floor. "Oh, jeez. Kerdik, it's alright. Thank you for being sweet to me, but this isn't how we run the household. You're all fine. I'm just a little out of sorts, I guess." They picked up their heads tentatively, but didn't rise. "Someone want to tell me what I missed in the last two days?"

Jean-Luc and Montel burst through the front door, panting at the news they needed to confirm with their eyes. Montel's mouth was agape at the sight of me. "Princess! You're injured! You're covered in blood! We thought you dead! The Untouchables have been going mad trying to find your body. Jean-Luc, do something!"

"*Where did he take you? How is it you're whole? It worked, then? Kerdik's blood healed you? Or did it make you worse off? I honestly can't tell with all the blood. Though, you're upright, so that's a definite benefit,*" Jean-Luc said in a flurry of words.

I nodded to Jean-Luc, but didn't answer aloud. The last thing I needed was people trying to attack Kerdik for the use of his blood. "Kerdik gave me some rare herbs, and basically did what you told him to do, Jean-Luc, and here I am."

Kerdik's arms tightened around me, no doubt miffed that I'd cheated him out of the almighty credit. "You've all seen her now, so go on about your business. She's not a fountain to be gawked at for your amusement."

"Please, someone tell me where my dad is. And what about Draper or Bastien? Has anyone seen them around?"

Montel motioned me toward him and Jean-Luc when the others scurried away without a word. "Come with us. We'll fill you in on everything you need to know. Let's go to the study."

I made to follow, but Kerdik held me tight. "She's not going to hold court dressed in a wet, bloody nightgown. You can explain things to her upstairs, where she can change into something people won't gawk at her in."

I obeyed, moving forward with Kerdik's arm around my waist. He kept me tucked tight to his side, not permitting an inch of space between us. I was worried at the unfocused state of the house, and it seemed Kerdik had the same misgivings. Something had happened while I was away, and until I had everyone back under the roof where I could see them, I wasn't going to be able to calm down.

We moved quickly up the stairs, though Kerdik held my elbow and my hand, escorting me as if I was fragile, and might fall without his support. My bare feet tiptoed on the stone steps, feeling cold with trepidation. When we entered my bedroom, my chest heaved to find Draper sitting up in the bed. His arms were the only ones I'd seen that I would leave Kerdik's for. I ran to my brother and jumped up on the mattress, crawling to him in my bloody nightgown so I could fling my arms around his neck.

"Rosie! You're alive?" He let out a grateful sob as we held each other. "The blood! So much of it. Jean-Luc, hurry! Do something!"

I kissed Draper's cheeks four times apiece before answering. "I'm not hurt. Kerdik saved my life. That's where we were. He took me so that I had time to heal up."

Draper cupped my cheeks, his eyes sparkling with moisture as he took in my face. "I wouldn't have survived if you'd died. Remember that."

I nodded, kissing his forehead before I realized that I was essentially pushing my bloody boobs in my brother's face. "Let me wash up and get dressed. You're okay, though?"

"Um, not really. Everyone's searching for you, readying

to fight, but my legs still aren't cooperating. I've been stuck here since I woke up." He stared at my shoulder, perplexed. "Your skin looks... different. Are you sure you're alright?"

"I've got my brother back. What more could a girl need?" I grabbed clean clothes while Kerdik slipped behind the partition to fill the tub for me. "So what'd I miss?"

Before anyone could explain what their reluctant covert glances meant, the bedroom door banged open, startling all of us. Kerdik ran out from behind the partition, his hands raised to dole out whatever magic could send a reckoning to the intruder. His arms deflated when he saw who it was. "Oh, you again."

I turned around and saw the most beautiful sight I could've hoped for. Bastien was unshaven, unshowered, flannel shirt untucked, and completely and totally perfect. His mouth fell open as he took me in from head to toe. He let out a bleat of anxiety, stumbling as he closed the distance between us. "Jean-Luc, help her! Rosie, how are you... Where are you hurt? I... but they told me your body was..." The words didn't matter anymore. Bastien crashed into me, forgetting our audience and kissing my lips the way they were meant to be seduced – stripped of all reserve. His arms around my waist tightened and lifted me so that my toes were two inches from the rug. His eyes squinched shut like he was in pain, and the moan he let out when he tasted my lips sounded equally agonized and relieved. I could feel his ache from our separation, and the elation at having me in his arms again. My *lueur* inside of him had kept him from finding rest, and had kept me from finding any sort of peace for very long, even in fake Heaven.

Link shut the door so that the household didn't see our reunion. "Welcome back from the dead, Rosie. I think our boy missed ye just a wee bit."

Bastien finally set my toes back on the floor when Draper and Link started whistling and catcalling at our display. He couldn't stop kissing my face, but finally pulled back when he caught sight of my one freaky peach eye. "Rosie, your eye! It's... Where did you take her?" he demanded of Kerdik.

Kerdik straightened with a sneer. "You'll watch your tone with me. I don't answer to you."

I turned to Montel, trying to assemble my bearings. "Montel, would you mind going down to the kitchen and waiting for the cook to put together some food for us? I've got to talk to the guys about some family stuff."

"Of course, your majesty." Montel bowed to me, which wasn't like him when we were on the wall together, but I knew Kerdik got people all turned around. Before he left, he met my eyes, startled when he noticed the wonky color. He recovered gracefully, swallowing his nerves when he parted with a, "I'm so glad you're well, and that you're home safe."

I smiled at him, and waited for the door to shut. Then I

let my shoulders drop and my body sag against Bastien's. It was a delicious relief to be near him. Couple that with the fact that I hadn't eaten in two whole days, and I was a little woozy from all the excitement.

"Easy, babe. Let's lie you down. What's all this blood from?"

"I'm not hurt at all. Better than new, actually." I shook my head. "Where's my dad, and where's Mad?"

"Madigan's gathering the army, and Dad's with a few men, knocking on every door to see if anyone knows anything about your disappearance." Draper pointed to the partition. "Wash up, and then start talking, little bird."

"*I'll help you in the bath. I need to check your injuries anyway.*"

"I promise you, Jean-Luc, there's not a scratch on me. I don't need help, but thank you. I'm just exhausted, hungry, and you know, glad to be home."

"I'll help her," Bastien insisted, not taking no for an answer. "What? She's my charge. I need to know if she's injured." His arm around me was firm and steady as he led me past Kerdik, who met my eye with silent agony that Bastien was going to see me naked in the tub he'd drawn for me.

I caught Kerdik's arm, pausing our slow progression to the partition. "Kerdik, would you mind explaining what you know to Jean-Luc and the others? I didn't tell him down there in front of everyone because I didn't want to make you a target."

Kerdik's nose scrunched. "What are you talking about? Who's foolish enough to target me?"

"People who find out your blood can bring people back from the brink of death. I don't want people attacking you for your blood, so the confession stays here."

Kerdik straightened in confusion. "You're trying to protect me? That's not how this works. *I* protect *you*."

"I think you need to learn a thing or two about me. I don't feed the people I love to the wolves."

Kerdik let a little of our secret rapture for each other slip through in his passionate stare. Then he disregarded Bastien's presence and reached out to touch my cheek. "I'll tell them everything they need to know. You go wash up."

Bastien led me away from Kerdik and behind the divider to our own private little hutch. It felt just separate enough for me to feel the heat of his stare, and still be able to hear Kerdik walk them through what they'd missed.

Bastien didn't say a word as he lifted my bloody nightgown over my head, and I didn't stop him. He kissed my lips, sending shivers through the both of us. His eyes poured over my body, trying to be clinical as he searched for abrasions on his charge, but he failed miserably. I could see the lust and feel his eyes caressing my curves. His voice came out in a husky whisper that made my knees tremble. "If your brother wasn't right out there, I would memorize every inch of your body with my tongue."

Kerdik's voice cut through our sexy moment with an

unforgiving sharpness. "Her brother might not be able to hear you, but I can."

"Good!" Bastien shot back without apology. He held my hand above my head, and turned me around in a slow twirl so he could see my body from every angle. I felt like a ballerina on a music box, beautiful and precious. It was a steep change from the disaster of the first time he'd seen me naked. His brows furrowed, and then he turned around so I could take off my underwear and step into the tub. "What's all this blood from?"

Kerdik explained with clinical detachment everything that had changed as a result of him giving me his blood. He conveniently left out the fact that I could kiss him now without breathing fire, for which I was grateful.

I washed myself thoroughly, scrubbing the dried blood that had caked between my fingers and streaked my body in cruel ribbons. I didn't want to confess my sin to Bastien, but knew that I couldn't take the adoring look in his eyes without telling him the truth. I wanted to deserve his affection, not lie to him to keep it. In a whisper that shook me, I said, "I thought I was dead when I woke up, that I was in some sort of afterlife. I didn't know I would be able to come back to you."

"Oh, that's terrible." Bastien's compassion made the guilt roil under my skin, and I knew I had to come clean before the deception ate me alive.

He still had his back to me, and somehow talking to the back of his head made the confession a little easier. I got out of the tub and worked the towel around my body, hoping my next words wouldn't push him away.

"When I thought I was dead, and a couple times when we weren't together, I kissed Kerdik. I didn't know, Bastien. I thought…"

Bastien turned around to face me. His eyes widened, his expression steeled, and then a few heartbeats later, his shoulders deflated. "It's okay. Even if you'd known, you were clear that we weren't back together yet. Stings, but I get it."

I mulled over the logic, grateful he'd come to it first. "I want to be together, now that you're not drunk, and I'm not dead."

Bastien met my gaze, and we searched each other for signs of flight. When he finally spoke, it was slow and quiet, his breath tickling my nose. "You and me, then. I'm in."

My heart swelled as my cheeks lifted in a smile that couldn't be contained. We'd been through so much just to get us to this place. I wanted to get closer, to forget the world and sink into his arms until the craziness stopped spinning.

Bastien kissed my lips once, inviting me in, instead of pushing me away. The stark contrast was not lost on me. He kissed my lips over and over, keeping our light moans muted so the others wouldn't know the tawdry things we were up to behind the partition. I mean, obviously they knew, but we tried to keep quiet all the same.

The scent of the stew I'd grown attached to was brought into the room, distracting me from the sensual moment when my stomach growled. Bastien's eyes were lidded when I pulled back from our kiss, stepping toward the stool to slide on my clothes. He wet his lips, and I could practically feel the desire rolling off him, matching my own. We were going to be in a whole heap of trouble if we weren't afforded a smidge more privacy than this.

When we rejoined the others, Kerdik had caught them up to speed, but I was still in the dark. "Anybody want to tell me what I missed while I was out?"

Draper's eyes darted to Link, who looked to the side to let us all know that he wasn't about to be the one dropping the bomb on my head. Draper rubbed the back of his neck, staring down at his knees on the mattress. "We lost four-hundred-thirty people while you were out. They didn't get the *guérison* elixir with a queen's touch because you couldn't get through everyone before the peludas attacked, so they succumbed to the poison and died." Draper paused only for my gasp of shock and guilt, but pressed on. "The peludas attacking our village were meant to take you out."

"I gathered as much when the whole herd surrounded me." I wanted to apologize for being unable to heal the people who had died, but I knew nothing I said would bring them back. Instead, I tried to focus on the problems that were still unfolding, putting off my self-flagellation for later. "Is Morgan up to her normal awesomeness again?"

Draper nodded. "I don't understand why she would try and kill you like that."

I shrugged, poking at a guess I'd been pondering. "I don't think it was supposed to kill me. I think she was testing my ability to hear unknown languages. Like, she knows I can talk to animals, but she didn't know if I could communicate with mutant creatures. Now, I guess she knows."

Draper's jaw dropped. "Those are some high stakes for an experiment."

"What else would you expect from a megalomaniac?" I scratched an itch on my elbow. "And did we find out who black cloaked dude was? Sluagh or something?"

Draper swallowed twice before words came to him. It was then that I noticed Bastien and Link were looking at their boots, avoiding my eyes at all costs. "A Sluagh is a spirit from Link's country, not Avalon. That one came here isn't good, Ro."

"You want to be more specific? He didn't look like a spirit. I mean, he touched me without his arm going straight through me. Did Morgan send the Sluagh guy after me?"

Link stretched out his collar as if it was too tight, and finally found his voice. "It's a spirit with a body. We – Mad and me – back when we first got out of our queen's army, do ye remember what I told ye we did?"

I nodded, recalling our conversation shared in the cell. "Yeah. You two got your Untouchable marks, and went to the compound Mad was trained in. You took out the young boys, locked the doors and lit the place up to stop them from making any more child soldiers."

Link bobbed his head, and waited a few more beats before the words came to him. I could tell Kerdik was growing impatient, but he waited out the tensed silence by moving to my other side. His hand rested on the small of my back, relaxing my posture while simultaneously stiffening Bastien's.

"No," Bastien ruled, taking the proverbial microphone from Link to highlight his personal vendetta. "You don't touch her there." He removed Kerdik's hand from my back as if it was a chewed piece of gum on my shirt.

Kerdik was livid. "I'd like to know when you thought your Untouchable status extended to me, worm."

Bastien didn't answer, but merely shrugged, as if to say that this was the way things would be, no matter who had more power in Avalon.

Kerdik studied Bastien's resolve, and then pfft'd in his face, deciding the buzzing fly wasn't worth the effort of swatting. "I'll do as I please, and being near Rosie pleases me."

I clapped my hands before the idiocy got out of hand. "Enough, both of you. I'm in both your lives, so best deal with it and get along. Bastien, Kerdik's my best friend, so suck it up. Kerdik, Bastien's my boyfriend now, which you knew was coming, so be cool. Moving on." My cheeks were warm, but I was determined not to lose what little ladylike demeanor I had at my disposal. This would not turn into Jerry Springer, so help me. "Link, you were saying."

Link rubbed the nape of his neck nervously. "When they died, a flock of ravens flew up from the smoke and bolted eastward in the sky. It... We didn't mean to... We didn't know."

Kerdik closed his eyes as if Link's incompetence pained him. "You and Madigan created an army of Sluaghs? You traded an army of men for an army of Sluaghs? Is this truly what you're telling me?"

Link hung his head in shame, while Bastien gaped at his friend. "Are you serious, Link?"

"Aye. Wish I wasn't. We set to killing all the Sluaghs we unleashed on Faîte. There were forty-eight soldiers, and we've killed forty-seven Sluaghs, if tha helps. But ye never know if there were more than we realized. We think there's only one left, but he's a bugger of a problem, tha last one. In the beginning, they were tracking Mad, I think." His voice dropped to just above a whisper. "Tha's how Meara died. The last Sluagh couldn't best him, so he targeted Mad's lady. Took her soul and then did... bad things with her body."

My hand flew over my mouth to stifle my gasp. I wanted to run to Mad and throw my arms around him. "Where is he? Is Mad alright?"

"Aye. Everyone knows it's a wasted effort to go after him. The Sluagh eventually learned the same."

I rubbed my temples, trying to sort out my confusion.

"Wait, back up. What the crap is a Sluagh? Like, textbook it for me."

Kerdik was patient as he turned to explain things to me, while everyone else's jaw remained on the floor. "A Sluagh is a Fae gone wrong. It's a wicked Fae that dies and comes back as a malicious spirit, whose mission is to suck out the souls from the living – souls of the good or the bad. Sluaghs aren't truly alive or dead, but each soul they steal makes them stronger. They become a collection of stolen souls." He turned to Link with a steely expression. "Your dear Link and his friend unleashed a slew of malevolent soul collectors on the world all at once." He paused and pinched the bridge of his nose. "And now this last one's after Madigan?"

Link nodded. "Tha looks to be the way of it. They tracked Mad for a while, and we dealt with them as they came. When the last one standing couldn't kill us, he went for Meara." Link shook his head. "She was a good lass. Didn't deserve what they did to her."

The pieces started to fall into place like slow-moving dominoes waiting for me to push them over. "But they're targeting me now. It was two separate attacks, then. The Sluagh guy is after me, and Morgan le Fae sent the peludas to kill me, too."

"Aye. The Sluagh's after ye because ye were engaged to Mad. There's only one nasty Sluagh left. We can't seem to get our hands on him, no matter how hard we try. He resurfaces a few times a year, but we manage to fend him off. Now tha we're rooted here, it's a bit more complicated."

"But I'm not Mad's fiancée anymore. Why didn't the last Sluagh dude lose interest?"

"Because they're manky spirits, Rosie. They don't see much reason." Link swallowed hard, his eyes on his boots. "Mad loves ye, so the last Sluagh will have your soul. Then he'll do what he likes with your body once he gets ye."

MORGAN'S BEST LAID PLANS

y mouth was dry, and my ears felt like they were filled with cotton. "They did stuff to Meara's dead body?" I finally asked, cutting through the many questions and accusations the men fired at each other.

"Mad was going crazy from the hunt for the last Sluagh, searching for Meara's body. When we found her..." Link looked out my window, seeing something that wasn't there, as if searching out a memory he'd blocked from his mind long ago. "I went to the pub to blow off some steam after seeing sweet Meara like tha. I didn't know Mad would call the Cheval Mallet while I was out. I was at the pub for a couple hours, and when I came home, he was gone."

Bastien's voice was tensed. "So now it's come here to kill Rosie and steal her soul?"

Link's chin touched his chest, his shame palpable. "I'm

sorry. I didn't think they'd follow us to Avalon. Sluaghs are only known to do their dark deeds in Éireland."

Kerdik's response was tart. "That's quite the oversight. Sluaghs stay mostly in Éireland because you have a colder climate, which the undead prefer. But they can travel and glean from anywhere they please. You brought chaos into Urien's home, and now there's a target on his daughter."

Link ran his hands through his honey-colored hair, messing the follicles and trying to find an answer that was both truthful and not damning. "Aye, but we didn't know the last Sluagh would track us here."

I swallowed hard, banding my arms around my waist. "So the last Sluagh's after me because he thinks Mad loves me?"

Link softened. "Mad does love ye. And yes, tha's what I can make of it. I didn't realize the cloaked man ye described was a Sluagh, but then I saw the ravens coming in from the west when ye were being attacked by the peludas. The ravens always come first. Then your cloaked man appeared, and there he was. I tried to kill him, Rosie, but I was also trying to keep ye from being eaten by the peludas."

I suddenly felt two hands on the small of my back, silently dueling for purchase on the coveted space. Kerdik and Bastien closed in on either side of me, as if they expected I might be snatched at in the next five seconds. "So he brought in the peluda monsters to finish me off?"

Draper fielded this one, his eyes darting to the guys

warily, warning them to be cool. "No, those were courtesy of Morgan. She tied a ransom note to one of the peludas' necks. The men found it after they'd slaughtered the beasts."

I pinched the bridge of my nose in consternation. "Super. So the Sluagh dude wants to kill me, *and* can activate Mad, the super soldier, to get at me. Add that to Morgan still being pissed that I have the jewels, plus a ton of her people. What's she holding over my head this time? She already let Demi get killed." Throwing out the horror so cavalierly made me wince, but just speaking the terrifying event aloud helped me name the beast, which made me hope that one day somehow I might get a little closure on it all. That was my theory, anyway.

Draper pursed his lips and blew out a loud breath of unconcealed nerves. "Before you get worked up, know that a small battalion's already forming. They're going without you, so promise me that you understand that you're to stay here."

My eyes rose up to the ceiling at the big brothering, but on the inside, my guts started to roil. "I'll be a good little princess and stay here. What's she threatening this time?"

I could practically hear the words before they came out of Draper's mouth, as if my whole world had been set up to break down into slow-motion. My mouth went dry and my palms started to sweat when Draper lowered his head. "Her soldiers intercepted Lane, Reyn, Damond and Remy on their way back from Lot's kingdom. She's holding them in her dungeon until you give up the jewels."

I didn't hear much else. I think I spaced out for a solid minute before my feet started moving of their own accord. I went to my wardrobe and shoved my toes into work boots, lacing them up without participating in the conversation in which Kerdik was asking question after question. It wasn't until my hand slipped on the doorknob that Link and Bastien came to life and stopped my progression by slamming the door shut and holding their hulking arms across the exit, so I couldn't get out. "Move, please," I requested quietly.

Bastien shook his head, his mood somber and respectful of my crushing agony that someone would snatch at my mom. "You know I can't do that, Daisy. You're staying here. The people need you. They just lost hundreds of their own from the poisoned wells. You have to stay here with Urien. We're going to try and extract Lane, Reyn, Remy, Damond and..." He cleared his throat, stopping himself short. "We're trying to get them out in secret. We just don't have the manpower to send in our men. Our guys are tradesmen, shepherds and farmers, for the most part; Morgan's got a whole army to defend herself with. We have to be smart."

Draper spoke up from the bed. "Duke Lot's sending a group of his fastest riders to meet our search party halfway, so we're not alone."

"Give Morgan the Jewels of Good Fortune," I ruled as I

whirled around, resolute that this would all end in the next five seconds. "Give her whatever she wants."

Draper was levelheaded when I was ready to go all kamikaze. "No. The welfare of the kingdom is worth more than one life – even Lane knows that. You can't betray your people. I know it comes from a good place, but it's not the right move. If you cave now, then Morgan knows all she has to do is keep abducting Lane, and you'll hand over whatever she's got her eye on. This is her first move in a series of moves to take control again. Trust me Ro, Morgan has no intention of giving Lane back. Even if you marched in there with all the missing jewels, she'd kill Lane right in front of you just to show you she can." Draper ran his hand over his face, his expression hard. "Though believe me, I had the same thought when I first found out. Dad had to knock a fair bit of sense into me."

Draper's logic was solid, but I didn't care. "Whatever. I'm going. If I can't figure out how to bust her, Reyn, Damond and Remy out, I'll trade myself for them. Morgan hates me most anyways. She'd go for it." I gulped when images of the torture I guessed she'd have in store for me plagued my vindictive imagination. *Whatever.* "Morgan can have me, but she can't have Lane. The world needs Lane."

Bastien wrapped me in a hug from behind, his lips pressing to my temple. "Remember that promise you just made your brother that you'd stay in the palace? It's still in effect. You're not going. You're staying right here."

My breath came in shallow pants as the many possibilities dawned on me, playing with my worst fears and showing them to me in various twisted forms. "I can't wait here like a chump while Lane's scared, Bastien! She puts up a good front, but she can't handle this! Her own sister holding her hostage?" I tried to wriggle out of Bastien's hug, but his arms tightened around my torso to ensure I didn't escape. "Let me go! Lane's my mother!"

Bastien barely jostled with my fight, so I implored my whole body to try and get myself free. My legs kicked up, and my head thrashed around wildly until Link came to his aid, the jag. Link sandwiched me with his arms hugging Bastien, so my face was pressed to his chest. "Settle, Rosie. I'll go with Bastien to make sure he comes back to ye in one piece."

Fear like none other lit me up from the inside. "No! No, Bastien can't go! That's exactly what she'll be hoping you'll do!" My shallow breaths were now on the verge of hyperventilating gasps as Link tightened his grip on Bastien's shoulders, squishing me so I couldn't knee him in the groin to escape. When my best fight wasn't enough, I wailed the name that sliced a tear through my unhealed heart. "Demi!" I felt Bastien stiffen, but I didn't stop. "She let Demi get beheaded because I loved him! She'll kill you, Bastien! There's no way that's not in her plan. You can't go! You can't! I can't go through that again! I can't hold your head in my hands like I held Demi in the well. I can't do it!"

Bastien had the nerve to coo at my anxiety, which morphed me into a ball of rage. I renewed my efforts to get away, and thrashed with unquenchable devotion to my desire to escape. "Hey, it's alright. I'm Untouchable. She can't hurt me, Daisy."

Tears sprang to my eyes, and though I should've been expecting the red goo to cloud my vision, I panicked anew when I couldn't breathe, and on top of it, couldn't see. Link jumped back from the horrific sight that was me bleeding from my tear ducts, the red drooling all down my face. He cried out, his hand over his mouth. "Jays! Somebody stop her! Rosie, no more!"

Though Kerdik had explained my body's new quirk, it was frightening all the way around. It wasn't until Kerdik shoved Link aside and brushed his fingers down my face that I quieted from shrieks of fear to mere whimpers of a girl on the verge. Water dripped from his fingertips, and he shushed me as he washed my face. "Darling, it's okay. Bastien's right; Morgan won't touch him. She can't. The rule of the Untouchables is the highest law in Avalon. Even if she ordered it, no soldier in his right mind would carry it out. And Bastien can handle the ones not in their right minds well enough."

Bastien was surprisingly calm. "He's right, Daisy. I have to get Reyn. I can't leave him to rot in Morgan's dungeon."

"You don't think Morgan knows that? You don't think she set this up as a trap? Come on, Bastien! You know she's trying to lure you in. What other possible use could Reyn have to her?"

Bastien leaned his forehead to the back of my head, and I could practically feel the agony radiating off of him. "She'll use Reyn to torment Lane. They publicly announced their engagement in Province 5 while visiting Lot. Morgan doesn't have any use for Reyn other than to take something precious from Lane and break it in front of her. That's how she works – it's what she did with you and Demi. I have to go get him."

I was shaking in Bastien's firm grip, his chest moving steadily against my back, while Kerdik stroked my cheeks with his wet fingers. "Let me come with you," I begged in a whisper. "I can be the bait. She'll trade me for the two of them, no problem. She'll probably even throw in Remy and Damond if we play our cards right."

Bastien placed a pained kiss to the nape of my neck. "It's like you don't know me at all. That you think I would trade you for the whole kingdom shows how little you get that I'm in deep for you. You're staying in this palace. If I have to tie you to a chair myself, I will."

I gasped, but Kerdik was unperturbed. "No need." Then he closed his eyes, held my face and murmured a string of syllables that sounded like evil sorcerer kind of gibberish. When he opened his eyes, he brought my wrists up between us and exhaled on the tender insides, giving me the shivers. "She won't involve herself now," Kerdik assured everyone. "She'll be staying inside the palace until I say so."

My upper lip curled in a sneer. "I'd like to know who you think you're talking to. I said I was going, so that's where I'll be. I'll send you a postcard when I get there."

Kerdik smiled at my sass, as if he found our bickering adorable, which only steamed me more. "You're bound with an *écrouer* charm, which means you won't be going anywhere. You won't be able to set foot outside the palace until I release you, which I have no intention of doing. This manic desire to throw yourself to the wolves needs to get out of your pretty little head."

I had a strong desire to run to the nearest exit, just to prove him wrong. "Let. Me. Go," I seethed, speaking to both men, who were just as stubborn as I was. It was one of the things I loved about them – their unbendable spirits, fierce and awe-inspiring. Now it was just plain pissing me off.

Kerdik acted as if I was a pouting five-year-old, his cheek dimpling with indulgence. He brushed a few stray curls from my face, ignoring my feral snarls that came through clenched teeth. "I'll see if I can't find this Sluagh who's haunting you. After I tear his soul-sucking body apart, I'll catch up with Bastien and the rescue team."

"I can handle the Sluagh," I claimed foolishly. I knew I was all talk; dude had already bested me twice now. I just couldn't stand the thought of Lane in the dungeon one more second. "Lane! You don't understand, because you don't need anybody. But I do. I need my mom. Please."

"How wrong you are to think I don't need you." He cupped my cheeks, ignoring Bastien's low growl, warning Kerdik that he was about six inches too close to me. "Your life comes first; everything else is a distant second." Then Kerdik took a chance with his immortal life, and leaned in to brush his lips to mine.

The pledge was so beautiful and precious, that I didn't pull away or lash out.

Bastien was not quite as tranquil. He moved me to the side and pulled back his fist to take a swing at Kerdik. Though Bastien was bigger, Kerdik was just plain more powerful. He caught Bastien's fist and tsked him, as if Bastien was a naughty boy. "My, my. You seem to forget your place, worm. Save your brute strength for freeing your friend and your love's mother. For her sake, I'll spare you my wrath today." Then with a ferocious glint to his eye, he warned, "Only today."

"You don't kiss my girlfriend and act like you get to walk away with your face intact. Rosie, do you want Kerdik to kiss you?"

I rubbed the nape of my neck with chagrin, confused as to how we'd gotten so off-topic. "I'm with Bastien now, Kerdik, so you can't kiss me anymore."

Kerdik's eyes narrowed. "I do as I please, and being near you pleases me. Now give your *lueur* to a Brownie you trust, and Bastien will be on his way."

My eyebrows furrowed. "Huh?"

"Give us a minute, guys," Bastien said to the others as he pulled me out into the hallway. He shut the door and tugged me into the next room, which was empty, and probably had been used as a guest room at one point or another. The lackluster bed had no posts, headboard or footboard, but it was nice enough, with a desk in the corner and emerald-colored silk tapestries to match the rest of the house. As soon as Bastien shut us in the room together, he heaved a breath of relief that we were finally alone. "There are too many people in our business. I can barely think." He came to himself a marginal amount and pointed his finger at me. "No more kissing other men. I don't care how immortal they are."

I lowered my chin in contrition. "I can get on board with that. What's this business about giving someone else my *lueur*? I don't like that idea."

"It's necessary, babe. I'm going to bust everyone out of Morgan's dungeon. I don't want to take your *lueur* that far from you again. That was awful, having part of you, but not all of you. I know it messed you up too, being divided like that. We need someone you trust who'll guard you, and who will also give back your *lueur* without a fight when I come home."

I shrugged, chewing on my lower lip as I stared at my boots. "I dunno. I mean, a few of the guys I work with on the wall are Brownies, I think. I prefer someone I already know. Someone we already trust. How do you feel about Montel?" I recalled my friend's light brown eyes.

Bastien's mouth drew to the side as he thought over my suggestion. "I could see that working. He's not exactly dead weight, though he's not a soldier, either."

"Draper trusts him to work next to me and walk me home at night. I wouldn't mind hanging with Montel for a while." When I met his eyes, I tried to communicate my plea quietly, since attempting to barrel my way out to get to Lane did nothing but get me incarcerated inside my own home. "I don't like you going off to Morgan's. She'll hurt you, Bastien."

Of all things, Bastien smiled. The corner of his mouth turned upward in time with his notched eyebrow, as if he thought a threat on his life was cute. "I'm going to make sure she can never get at you again. I'm taking Mad with me, and we're putting an end to her."

My intake of breath probably shouldn't have happened, but there it was all the same. My boyfriend wanted to murder my biological mother, and part of me thought that was a good idea. I hung my head in shame. "What kind of a person does it make me that I'm mostly okay with you putting down my birth mother?"

Bastien reached out to stroke my hip, tethering me to him when I felt on the edge of drifting off into my own abyss. "The kind of person who has true goodness in her, plus an evil mother." He leaned his forehead to mine, his hands moving around my torso in a loose hug that kept me centered. "Tell me not to kill Morgan."

I considered his plea, and after a few beats, obliged. "Please, Bastien. Don't kill my mother."

He kissed my lips once, softly and so quietly, it felt like we were trying to hide a secret from the empty room. "I have to, Daisy. Avalon can't unite with her on the throne, and I can't let it slide that she attacked Lane, Reyn, Damond, Remy, and..." He cleared his throat. "You tried to stop me just now, so your conscience is clear. I'm acting on my own with this, and there's nothing you can do about it."

I blinked up at him, stunned at the lengths he went to so that I could sleep at night. My arms slowly coiled around his neck so I could hug him, while standing on my toes. My stomach pressed to his, and my cheek rested against the scruff I loved the look and the feel of. "You love me. I see what you're doing, and thank you."

His finger traced the slope of my arm. "Your skin is different now. Does it feel different?"

"Not really. The crying thing is terrifying. Might take me a while to get used to that." I pursed my lips, not wanting to ask the next question, but part of me needed to know. "I haven't seen my weird eye yet. Is it..." My palms started to sweat, and I fought to keep myself from freaking out. I'd grown up with a lazy eye, and since it was fixed and pointing in the right direction, looking normal had spoiled me. I didn't want my eyes to do funky things again. I knew how that could ostracize a person.

Bastien thumbed my chin and took his time studying one eye, and then the other. "I think it's cool."

I squinched my eyes shut and nodded my gratitude. "Are they pointing in the same direction?"

I didn't expect Bastien to swat my butt during my vulnerable moment. His large palm whapped a squeak out of me. My lashes flew open as I frowned up at him.

"Sorry," Bastien said with an impish grin. "You had your eyes closed, so I had to double-check. Yep, they're both pointing in the same direction."

I grumbled, shaking my head at his boyishness that still managed to surface, even in such dire times. "I hope you enjoyed that one. It'll be your last for a while."

Bastien reached both hands around and started drumming a rhythm on my butt as he spoke, taking full advantage of our alone time. "I'll leave Link with you to help Kerdik look for the Sluagh. I'm thinking I should take Mad, so the Sluagh can't trigger him to kill you."

"Sounds like a solid plan." I stiffened against him as an errant part of my brain clicked a missing puzzle piece into place. "Wait a second, you can't kill my mom."

His percussion on my backside stilled. "I can, and there's nothing you can do to stop me."

29

TAKING WHAT'S MINE

Bastien thought I was still playing around, but I wasn't. "Hold up. I need Kerdik for a second."

Bastien harrumphed. "Yes, please always tell me about your need for Kerdik while you're in my arms, and I'm squeezing your butt."

I sniggered and slid out of his embrace. "Seriously. Hold off on your murderous rage for five minutes."

I darted into the hallway and popped my head into the bedroom, where Kerdik was interrogating Link on anything he could tell him about the Sluagh. "Hey, Kerdik. I need you for a second." I couldn't very well have Bastien try to kill Morgan, when that feat was impossible by anyone other than the Daughters of Avalon. I wasn't sure if I was allowed to tell Bastien that secret, but he needed to know nonetheless.

Kerdik's wide mouth pulled into a relaxed smile when he took in my face – like the mere act of me entering the room made him more at ease. His eyes turned from no-nonsense when he'd been focused on getting to the bottom of things with Link, to softening when he took in my face. His shoulders rolled back, and the antagonism that was always just below the surface seemed to melt away when both halves of our strange friendship were united in the same room. "I hope it's for something unseemly."

I rolled my eyes at him. "Nothing like that. I..." My next words died on my tongue. I couldn't remember what I was going to say, or why it was important. I couldn't think about anything when my eyes fell to the table off to the side of my bedroom. I hadn't noticed them before, though now that I was staring at them, gaping like a fish, it felt like they came with their own horns, flashing lights and alarms.

Judah loved his Buddy Holly glasses. He'd had giant gold wire-rimmed ones in elementary school, but he used his tutoring money in the fifth grade that Lane paid him, and saved up for a new pair of glasses. Most kids were spending their allowance money on candy and cell phone apps. Judah wanted better glasses that helped him look like the tech geek he'd always wanted to be. When he outgrew them, he got the exact same pair in an adult size. Only I ever saw him without his glasses on in the morning

– his thick black rims lying on our nightstand next to my glass of water and whatever book he'd been reading to me that night.

"My love, what is it?" Kerdik asked, his brow furrowed at my instant state of shock. Draper and Link both hissed disapprovingly at his doting address, but they couldn't exactly correct the powerful immortal. He followed my gaze to the table, frowning in confusion. "What are these?" He picked up the glasses that were just lying there for anyone to touch.

It never even dawned on me that I'd not seen anyone in Avalon with glasses. Maybe they didn't have the technology, or perhaps they just didn't have poor eyesight here. "G-g-glasses," I stuttered, trying to find the right words. "Draper?" I asked, begging my brother for an explanation.

Draper's face turned stony. "I wanted to wait until Dad came home to tell you, but I guess now that Master Kerdik's sealed you in the castle, I can tell you the rest." He cleared his throat twice, working up the gumption to say his piece. "Morgan sent the ransom note around the peluda's neck, warning us to hand over the jewels if we wanted Lane and the others back." He kept his eyes on his hands, and I could tell he wished his body was fully functional again, so he could bolt out of the room and not get stuck with the short end of the stick. He didn't want to have to tell me the truth about the darker parts of life. "In her dungeon, Morgan has Lane, Reyn, Remy, Damond, and your friend from Common. She sent us a token from him, so you'd know she wasn't messing around."

My heart pounded so loud, I thought for sure all other sounds in the world must've gone mute under the weight of my touchstone crumbling to pieces. "The note," I demanded, my voice cracking. "I need to see that note. Do you have it?"

Kerdik picked up the piece of parchment that rested on the quaint, round table. Instead of waiting for him to read it to me, I moved across the room and took it from his hands, my fingers shaking as my eyes poured over the page. I had to see the crime for myself, to confirm beyond a shadow of a doubt that the worst of it all had come true.

Trepidation trembled in my lower lip as my eyes tried to make sense of the page. I don't know why I expected extreme duress to make me better at the thing I was no good at, but when the words didn't make themselves any clearer, frustration flared up in me over the limitation I'd accepted about myself long ago. My fingers trembled, and I knew all eyes were on me, watching my slow death and impending panic attack.

"I can read it to you," Draper offered, his voice gentle.

"No!" I snapped – more at the paper than at him. "I can figure this out. I need to read this for myself."

Link quirked his eyebrow at the guys. "Why would ye need to read it for her? She can see the threat plain as day."

I froze, realizing that perhaps Bastien had been a decent guy and kept my limitations private. I'd assumed Link and Mad knew about my dyslexia by now. I let Draper explain the situation to Link while I tried to make heads or tails of the note. "Why do people write in cursive?" I shouted, losing my temper and my grip on the world all at once. Cursive was my nemesis, throwing me off with all of its loops and curls that only complicated everything. Life was better with straight, definable lines you could depend on. Cursive did what it friggin' felt like, mocking me with its effortless elegance that I would never have. "'I p…'" I shook my head. "No. 'I ho-ha-ha-hap-hab-hab-habu-habu…'"

Kerdik came up behind me, quiet as I suffered through a waking nightmare my own imagination wasn't even cruel enough to conjure. "Come here," he offered, moving us toward the table and pulling me to sit on his lap. He rubbed my back in soothing circles, and then wrapped an arm around my waist as Bastien came into the room. Bastien's jaw clenched that I'd found out about Judah – or maybe it was because I was sitting on Kerdik's lap. Kerdik took the page from my hand and kissed my cheek. In a steady voice that didn't allow for any confusion, he read aloud for the room to hear Morgan's victory in kidnapping Judah, Lane, Reyn, Damond and Remy. She would exchange one of them for each jewel I brought back to her, and every day I delayed would be another they would remain in her dungeon, at the mercy of her merciless soldiers.

Tears were streaming down my face so fast that Bastien could barely dab them away before my jeans were sprinkled with droplets of blood. He leaned down and kissed my forehead. "Don't worry about it another second. I'll get them and bring them home."

It was a promise I needed, but one I was too familiar with the lows of Avalon to believe. "Judah's not built for Avalon. He can't handle a legit dungeon! He's supposed to be in school, studying and getting his degree. He's... Bastien, be careful with him. He's not an athlete or a soldier or anything like someone who can survive this kind of world."

Bastien tucked a curl behind my ear and wiped a streak of red across my face with his sweaty bandana, which was now ruined. "I won't break the people you love. But you have to do me a favor while I'm gone, okay? I need you to stay with Link. I mean, morning, noon and night, make sure he knows where you're at."

Kerdik's hand on my back was a comfort. "She won't be going anywhere, so Link can help me track down the Sluagh."

"Help me up," Draper requested, sliding his legs off the bed. Link hoisted him up and let him lean when he was unstable. "I'm going with you, Bastien. Lane's my mother." His conviction was so resolute that no one bothered to argue with him. I wanted Draper to stay home with me, but I couldn't begrudge him the freedom to do what Kerdik wouldn't let me.

"Please," I begged Kerdik quietly, while Bastien stood and started to go over the extraction plan with Draper. "Please let me go. Judah's my..." I gripped the t-shirt material over my heart, because the words were running out.

"I know. Though you have the kind of compassionate disposition that would throw herself in front of a chariot if it saved a mouse, so I'm not sure how serious to take your little tirades."

I didn't respond, but merely lived in my nightmare while Kerdik held me on his lap. Eventually I stood and started pacing the room, picking a different point of concern that I could address. "Bastien's going to try to kill Morgan."

Kerdik's voice turned sharp. "Bastien, you can't kill Morgan. I've made it impossible for anyone to murder the Daughters of Avalon, except for the Daughters of Avalon themselves. Not even I can do it." He paused for the gasps that echoed around the room, but then pressed on. "That information stays in here. Only Rosie was trusted enough to know that, but I can't very well have you going off to kill Morgan if you can't actually do it, Bastien. Lane can end Morgan. So free her and the others my darling requires. Protect Lane until she kills Morgan, then bring everyone home."

Bastien's nostrils flared in time with his finger-jab at Kerdik. "She's not your 'darling'. I could go my whole life without that kinda talk coming from you about *my* girl-friend." He pursed his lips, and then deflated. "And, you know, thanks. That's helpful information. How do you know that about the Daughters of Avalon?"

Kerdik's jaw clenched. "I know that because I was foolish enough to fix them with that protection. Urien knew of my temper, and how vexing the Daughters of Avalon could be, so he asked me to seal them against my wrath. I went one further to add protection against all foes they might come across. So no one can deliver the final blow to any of them, except for a Daughter of Avalon. It simply wouldn't work if you tried. They can die from each other's hands, an accident, a natural disaster, animal attack, or old age. That's all."

"And they don't know this about themselves?"

"No. I only trusted Rosie with that knowledge, and she came straight to me when you said you wanted to kill Morgan yourself."

Something about the way Kerdik said "she came straight to me" came with a snide undercurrent I didn't miss, but chose not to comment on.

Bastien shot me a warning glare, letting me know he was on his last nerve with Kerdik. "Fine. I'll give the *lueur* to Montel on my way out, and send him in to watch over you once he's ready."

I tried one last time to get Kerdik to revisit the terms of my incarceration. "Please, Kerdik. Please let me out."

"Not if you took off all your clothes and begged me on your knees. I'll not let you set foot in Morgan's dungeon."

"Talk about her naked again, and see what happens!" Bastien shouted, his temper rising like a balloon in danger of bursting. He took an ominous step in Kerdik's direction, and as if in slow motion, Kerdik rose ominously from his chair, chest puffed.

I ran to stand between the two bulls, my arms outstretched to stave off their stupidity. "Knock it off! Bastien, go do your thing. I can handle it. And Kerdik? You know you're just trying to get a rise out of Bastien. You want what's best for me? Then focus on more important things than this." I half-expected one of them to stick out their tongue at the other, but luckily, they seemed to have reached their maximum on childish behavior. "Lane, Judah, Reyn, Damond and Remy are suffering through who knows what, so all bickering can take a backseat to actual rescuing work."

Link nodded, following my example of getting back on track. "Aye. I'll go out as soon as your new *Guardien* comes in, and I'll scout out the border to see if I get any signs of the Sluagh."

"I'll wait with her until her new *Guardien* comes," Kerdik offered, and though he could've said it with a jeer at Bastien, he chose not to. Kerdik was actually trying to be a team player, interacting and being part of something, instead of always being above it. My shoulders lowered as I gazed on him with appreciation. Then he met Draper's eyes, swearing a vow of protection to my brother. "Nothing will harm your sister while I'm around."

Draper nodded, his fingers fumbling with his boots as he tried to slide them on his unsteady feet. "Let's go, Bastien. We need to meet Lot's riders soon."

Bastien pulled on my arm and led me out into the hallway, so we could have the illusion of privacy. "I want you with Montel or Link the entire time. Promise me. Even if Kerdik lets you out, don't come after us. I need you safe for like, a solid two weeks."

I nodded, glum in my defeat that I couldn't be of any actual use. "Be careful," I said lamely. There were so many cooler things I could've and should've said before we parted, but my heart was too unsteady in my chest. My insides hopped from worried to pissed to scared to defiant, bereft of all the right words.

"Tell me you love me," Bastien said with a small smirk, seeming to see my limitations and meet me halfway.

"I love you."

"Tell me you won't kiss Kerdik while I'm gone."

"I won't kiss anyone while you're gone. Except maybe Pascal. He's yummy."

Bastien's playful growl at the notion that I might take up with Montel's mid-sixties father was adorable. Then my boyfriend leaned in and brushed a slow kiss to my lips, nuzzling his nose to mine so we could breathe in the scent of each other's skin. I loved the smell of Bastien. "Tell me that when I come home with everyone, and the job's done, we can talk about where we'll land after Avalon's settled. You and me together, where we'll go when the dust clears. Tell me we can talk about where our home will be."

I swallowed, and after a few beats, nodded through my flabbergast. "Um, okay. We can talk about that. I don't totally know how that conversation's going to go, but sure."

He kissed me again, smiling at how dumbfounded I was at his declaration of permanence. "I love you, Daisy." Then he called into the bedroom, "Let's hit the road, Draper. She's about to wear me down and make me stay here."

I said nothing when I kissed my brother's cheek, and sent them off to find the missing pieces of my heart. I said nothing when Bastien made his way to Montel, to let him know that he had been chosen to be my temporary *Guardien*. I said nothing when my dad came back up and demanded to know how I was alive, and what had happened when Kerdik took my mangled body away, but let Kerdik explain it all. I said nothing when Link smooched my lips before he left to go scout out the province for the dreaded Sluagh. I said nothing when Kerdik brushed his knuckles to my cheek, giving up on trying to make conversation with me. I drank the tea he made me in silence. The two of us sat at the quaint table in my bedroom, like two old friends who had been through too many wars together, and didn't have the will to fill the silences of life with useless words.

I said nothing at all as the house emptied. I simply

stared out the window and waited with an ache in my chest, hoping that my family would come home unscathed.

Love the book? Leave a review.

Otherwise, Levi dies.

At this point in the story, I have no qualms.

30

UNTOUCHABLE GIRL

Enjoy a free preview of *Untouchable Girl*,
book six in the Faîte Falling series.

I don't care what anyone tells you, two weeks is an eternity to wait for your mom to come home to you. Lane had been gone for so long already, searching out allies in the withering provinces and inviting them to share in our newfound wealth. Stealing half the jewels back from Morgan was a scandal no one took lightly. Refugees from all over Avalon were still pouring in to stake their claims on a plot of land that wasn't under Morgan le Fae's rule.

Bastien was still gone, and if Kerdik hadn't magicked the castle to keep me locked inside, I would've gone along to help free Lane, Damond, Reyn, Remy, and… My fragile optimism always waned on that last one. The thought of Judah being held in a dungeon was a mental image I couldn't deal with if I wanted to keep my sanity. Judah had been my favorite (and often only) friend from grade school on, and deserved the best out of life. I'm talking parades, scholarships, hip-hop songs rapped in his honor – the works. What he did not deserve was to get caught up in my mess, and land himself smack in the middle of my mom's dungeon, without his glasses, and without me. I could picture him huddling in a corner with Lane, scared and cold. The image woke me up in the middle of the night, wracking me with fear. Then came the crash of self-loathing when I remembered I couldn't break myself out of the castle and go get him myself.

I frowned when a knock came to my bedroom door. I knew it was Kerdik, and I was still miffed at him for cutting me off from the rescue team. I took my sweet time opening the door, and shot daggers at him with my eyes when he greeted me with an irritable expression. "Took you long enough."

"If I haven't told you before, your personality is absolutely bursting with fruit flavor." I rolled my eyes at him, my hand on my hip. "Are you here to check that I haven't made an escape rope out of old sheets and flung them out the window, Warden?"

"If you were capable of besting my spellwork, then that's exactly what I'd be doing. As you can't even step a toe out of the castle, I'm not too concerned. I've brought you a friend to help you sleep."

The raccoon in his arms was grousing worse than me, and looked about an inch from biting into Kerdik's juicy forearm just to have done with it. "Hey, Walter," I greeted him without enthusiasm. Walter was a sourpuss, who had nothing good to say about the world. Montel wasn't too keen on me sleeping with another bear, so he thought a smaller animal would be best. Walter was a bit of a jerk, though, and we spent most of our time being pissed at each other. "I said, 'Hey, Walter.'"

"Do you really need to talk all the time?"

"Well, seeing as how that's what you're here for, yes."

"You're exhausting."

I sighed up at Kerdik. "Remind me again why I can't just have my birds? They'll knock me out so much quicker with all their chatter."

"Because the Sluagh can change himself into a raven. We can't chance him mingling with the other birds and flying his way straight inside."

"Still no sign of the Grim Reaper, eh?" A Sluagh was a wicked person who'd died, and his spirit was so evil that a Sluagh was formed. The nasty bugger roams about, trying to suck the souls from the dying, adding to its power with each conquest. As I understood it, these jaggoffs were usually only in Éireland, but this dude made a special trip overseas just for Madigan. The Sluagh was targeting me now, courtesy of my fake engagement to Mad.

Kerdik sighed at my appearance. "What are you wearing?"

I looked down and rolled up the sleeves of the shirt that hung down almost to my knees. "What? I'm allowed to wear my boyfriend's flannel shirts as pajamas. They're comfortable. I can look however I want in my own bedroom."

Kerdik's disapproving expression wasn't all that uncommon this week. He always had a bug up his butt about something. "I don't like the look of you in his clothes. Have Montel and Link seen you like this?"

"Of course not. Link prefers me in nothing at all, so that's how I greet him every morning."

Kerdik pursed his lips, unamused by my pretty funny joke. "Hilarious."

I crossed my arms over my chest and moved over to my window, unwilling to play this game for a third night in a row. "I'm sorry you can't find the Sluagh. I know you get moody when you lose."

He stood straighter, affronted. "I didn't lose. I'll find the Sluagh and make it suffer for forcing me to run around like a Commoner, searching for his own tail."

"Ugh. This guy. He's so annoying."

"Hush, Walter. Kerdik's just in a mood."

Kerdik's shoulders were tight as he stalked over to me. "I despise when you talk about me as if I'm a child."

"If you don't want to be treated like a child, then stop acting like a petulant baby."

Kerdik let out a noise of frustration. "You drive me crazy!"

"Me? You're the one who locked me inside, when I could be helping Bastien and the guys find Lane. At the very least, I could be helping the crew build the wall."

"I have half a mind to raise up the rest of the wall myself, just to have done with it."

I gaped at him. "Could you really do that?"

He shot me a simpering expression. "You must be joking."

I ran my fingers over Walter's fur, and he hissed for me to knock it off. "I guess that never dawned on me."

"Oh, sweet girl. Your mind is so limited when it comes to all I can do."

I scowled at him, looking more like the surly Walter than a girl should have a right to. "Don't call me 'sweet girl' when you're really saying 'you dummy'. It's patronizing." When we reached our usual nostril-flaring stalemate, I lowered my shoulders and fished for a lighter topic. "Where's Montel?"

"Doing a perimeter check before he turns in to sleep."

Montel was a nervous sleeper, which wasn't helped by the fact that Link made a big deal the first night about no man sharing a bed with an Untouchable's woman. I wasn't going to invite Montel into my bed in the first place, but the air had gone awkward all the same. "Okay. Did you need something?"

"A lock of your hair, actually."

I quirked my eyebrow at him. "Come again?"

He gave me a labored sigh, as if my simple query was an arduous give-me-a-break. "Do you really want the complicated explanation, or can I just say that it'll help me find the Sluagh, and be done with it?"

"If I'm donating body parts, I think I'll request the complicated explanation."

A labored sigh escaped his lips, complete with an eyeroll. "Every now and then, I wish you were afraid of me, like everyone else is. Then I wouldn't have to do taxing things, like explain myself." Kerdik harrumphed, as if my request was a huge inconvenience. "The Sluagh found you in Avalon, even though he's from Éireland. I want to know if it's you he's tracking now, or if it's still Madigan he's after. If he's tracking you, I can use the line of magic he's tapping to trace it back to him."

"Huh. Okay, then that's cool. See? Was that so hard to tell me?" I cast around for scissors, but didn't see any.

Kerdik pulled a pair from his back pocket. They were long and looked more like shears for sheep or something, which I guess it's possible they were. He made his way over to me and inspected my hair, as if one chunk would be more ideal for the magic than the others. "This one," he said, lifting up a curl to examine. It was a perfect Shirly Temple curl, unadulterated by a hairbrush or life. I didn't have a ton of perfect curls, but guessed donating one of them to save my life wouldn't be too grand a sacrifice. He pulled a string from the pocket of his standard brown pressed trousers and tied off the curl at the root. "Hold still."

The look on Kerdik's face when he examined my hair in his hand made me soften. He snipped the curl, not taking his eyes from the milk chocolate color I'd long been unimpressed by. Seeing my hair through his eyes was a new wonder, and I appreciated anew that there were parts of me that were beautiful. I'd been the stupid and ugly girl most of my life. The little looks of rapture that Kerdik or Bastien often shot me still took me off-guard.

A soft smile played on my lips. "Thank you."

Kerdik quirked his eyebrow at me. "For taking your hair? You're welcome?"

"No, for looking at it like that. Made me feel pretty just then."

Kerdik chuckled, and I loved the way his eyes crinkled in the corners. Something about the green skin made the delicate folds that much more intriguing. "Well, you are pretty, so I'm not sure I did anything miraculous, other than notice what's right in front of my face."

"Just mate already and be done with it," Walter sneered.

Continue the series,
and order *Untouchable Girl* today!

ABOUT THE AUTHOR

USA Today bestselling author Mary E. Twomey lives in Michigan with her three adorable children. She enjoys reading, writing, vegetarian cooking, and telling her children fantastic stories about wombats.

While she loves writing fantasy, dystopian, and paranormal tales for her readers, Mary also writes romance under the name Tuesday Embers, and cozy mysteries under the name Molly Maple.

Visit her online at www.maryetwomey.com, and sign up for her newsletter, so you never miss a new release.